Beast Unburdened

Robin O'Connor

Cover design: Robin's awesome husband

Princely Gates Publishing

For my husband,
always telling me I can do it.

ACKNOWLEDGMENTS

I'm kicking this section off by thanking my amazing husband for his endless patience and support. Not only did he help me keep going, read all my drafts and help me talk things over when I got stuck somewhere, he also created and designed the amazing cover art! (Listening to each of my picky demands and somehow making it work!)

Next, I want to thank my mom for her support, reading it and giving her honest opinion and her never wavering faith in me that I could do this. My brother for asking me if he could read it too and my dad for always quietly making me feel like I had already succeeded.

I want to thank my beta-readers for their help too. Ilona, you sent me so many emails, your attention to detail was amazing! And Miranda, your honest opinion meant the world to me. Of course, I have to mention Sanne, you were always so poetic in your feedback, it was beautiful!

TABLE OF CONTENTS

CHAPTER 1

Abigail

I was shaking with cold; utterly and completely frozen to the bone. I noticed it first thing when I woke up. It took a while before my brain rallied enough to pay attention to anything other than that terrible, bone-rattling cold. The second thing I noticed, was that I was most assuredly not in my cozy bedroom with its marvelous queen-sized bed with memory foam mattress.

It did not smell like my lavender detergent here, instead, the air was stale and musty. Although it was pitch black even with my eyes open as far as they could go, I could tell that I was in what amounted to a coffin made of glass. There was a glimmer above my head. Fear and panic bubbled through my bloodstream and I wanted to scream for help. I wanted to pound against the glass but I was shaking so badly from the pervasive cold I couldn't get a single muscle, not even my vocal cords, to obey.

Shit, shit, shit! This was a nightmare! This had to be a nightmare! But something told me that it wasn't, this was real. Trying to make sense of it all I worried I'd somehow died in my sleep or maybe slipped into some kind of coma and got mistaken for dead, and then I'd been buried. That was a thing right? Didn't I read somewhere that sometimes, though rarely, doctors mistakenly pronounced someone dead?

The air around me was warming a little and as it did my shaking subsided slowly until I could finally better sense my own skin instead of the numbness that had invaded my body. I was dressed, a relief for sure, in my suit from work. *What idiot had decided to bury me in my work clothes?* That was the last thing I wanted! If I never saw another day at my bank teller job again I'd be forever grateful.

Moving my head I could tell the two rubber bands I'd used on my last workday to restrain my thick, curly hair were still there. I'd used the makeshift solution because my favorite hairband had given out halfway through my work shift. What did that tell me? Whatever had happened to me must have happened right after work, or I'd have gotten home and changed my clothes.

Moving my hands to touch the glass just above me, I felt something dangle from my wrists. Wires stuck to my skin like the kind of electrodes from a medical exam. Now that I was aware I felt more of them attached to my chest, tucked into my blouse, and a pair attached to my temples and the sides of my neck. I yanked them off with a shiver as if they were cobwebs. *What the hell was this?*

This wasn't a coffin, was it? Why would they hook me up to electrodes inside a coffin? My brain tried to come up with logical explanations and settled on a CT scan or MRI, those were like a tube or something they stuck you in weren't they? Did I get into a car accident and didn't remember?

Then, from one moment to the next, light suddenly permeated the tiny space I was crammed into. It seared my eyes and blinded me. I was yanked from my resting place by rough, sandpaper-textured hands until I dropped to a hard metal floor. Guttural, male voices were talking around me but I couldn't understand a word they were saying.

When my eyes finally adjusted I wished immediately that they hadn't. I had landed in a nightmare, it was the only conclusion I could draw. The room around me was bright white and decked out with futuristic displays with blinking lights. There was a terrifying-looking mechanical arm tucked in behind a glass panel against one wall, right beside a medical cot of some kind.

Antiseptic smells singed my nostrils, making it at once clear this was indeed a medical room. Only it looked like something out of a sci-fi. Then there were the nightmarish-looking, wart-faced men looming around me. Big and hulking with gray skin and tusks, they looked to me like someone had crossed a Klingon with a warthog, with disastrous results.

One of them yanked me roughly off the floor and threw me onto the medical cot. I nearly rolled off on the other side, only stopped by the fact the bed rail on that side was raised. I screamed though, I couldn't help it, that thing was hideous and his grip had hurt my upper arm. That more than accounted for the pinch to prove this wasn't a dream. *Shit, shit, and double shit! What the hell was going on?*

I tried not to let another round of panic overcome me, I had to stay focused, and I had to find out what was going on. Except it was really hard when these ugly gray fuckers were looming around me looking menacing and talking in an indecipherable guttural language.

Futuristic medical-looking room, alien creatures, was I on a spaceship? About to be probed? *Holy crap had I lost my mind completely or what?* I knew I needed to get a grip but I couldn't seem to control my hyperventilating. As I struggled against the grip of the one pinning me to the medical cot there was excited talking among the others; something that sounded like orders being barked.

A new alien stepped into my field of view then, this one stunningly beautiful if terrifying looking in its otherness. Anthracite-colored skin shimmered and glittered, while long, straight black hair draped around broad shoulders clad in white. Through the hair poked sharply pointed ears with silver rings and studs glinting against the dark skin.

It was his eyes though that freaked me out. They were like shimmering black mirrors, not a speck of white, not even an iris or pupil visible. Just a sheet of glimmering black that reflected everything like mirrors. It was truly terrifying to look at. Those eyes were the kind of eyes they put on demons in movies or TV shows. They were truly evil.

Shaking I felt my body give in to the freeze part of fight, flight, or freeze; all of my muscles turning to stone. They were talking to the evil-looking doctor alien in harsh tones and then he pulled a tray of tools to him and approached me. *Was that a scalpel? Fuck no!*

When I struggled again the warthog aliens jumped into action, strapping me down to the medical bed until I couldn't move an inch. The shimmering black alien leaned over me and I couldn't keep looking when the scalpel approached my face. I squeezed my eyes shut tight. Briefly, I fought to keep my head straight when the alien grabbed my face and pressed down so my ear was pointing up.

Hot searing pain shot through me when the knife touched the skin just behind my ear. *Oh god, what were they doing to me?* It seemed far too long that the alien was rooting around behind my ear with his knife and god knows what else. It was searing pain and freezing cold and I screamed and screamed until my throat was raw and I tasted blood.

The pain eased when some cool gel was smeared across the incision and then my head was turned and the whole process started again on my other ear. My voice gave out halfway through that side but to my shock, as the sound of my screaming faded I realized I could hear the guttural voices of the aliens around me and now their words made sense.

"I love how she screams, such a pretty sound," one was saying as he elbowed the ugly brute next to him. "Oh yeah," that one replied and he made a lewd gesture, "Too bad she's worth more intact."

The anthracite alien above me smeared cool gel behind my ear and the pain faded away. His large but fine-fingered hand lifted away from pinning my head in place. I twisted to better see the room and he spoke to me, his voice low and mournful, pitched so the gray-skinned warthogs couldn't hear him. "I'm so sorry, little human. They don't waste painkillers on slaves. Please forgive me." His voice was perhaps the most gentle thing I'd ever heard, so sad and apologetic.

"Are you done yet, Doc?" demanded one of them and the doctor who'd just done surgery on my ears shook his head. "I need to do another check to make sure everything's healthy before I give her the fertility drugs you wanted."

"Well hurry up!" was the response from the mangiest and small looking of the four ugly aliens. "Oh shut it Frek!" the largest one responded, "You were against spending credits on those faulty pods!" The huge monster gestured at the glass pod they'd pulled me out of propped in a corner. "And now you're invested because it worked?"

Everyone but Frek laughed, a creaking, sharp sound that had me flinching back into the medical cot I was on. It was at that moment that the doctor leaned over me, his hand pressing something into mine, which was hidden from the others behind my leg. "Bide your time, please try to survive. You can't fight the Krektar. Not alone."

It was the scalpel, still bloody from his surgery on me. I tucked it away into my pocket, hoping it wasn't going to slice open my leg. Why was this doctor giving me a weapon? Apologizing? And advising me against the ugly gray creatures?

I didn't get it until one of the Krektar, the huge one, approached and snapped a collar around my throat. It was a black metal band with a small box with lights attached to it. He pointed at an identical one around the doctor's throat, "Listen, little slave, this is a pain collar." He held up a small remote, "One flick of this button and this is what happens." The ugly creature then pointed the remote at the doctor and with a mean grin turned it on.

Immediately, the anthracite-colored male grunted, his

eyes scrunching closed while his whole body tensed up. Then he dropped to his knees and only just caught himself on clenched fists; his entire body shaking with pain. He didn't immediately start screaming but as the Krektar appeared to dial it up the doctor lost the fight. He screamed out hoarsely before biting down hard on his bottom lip with teeth far too sharp to be human until he bled red blood in a puddle on the metal floor in front of him.

I stared in horror, torn between abject fear for myself and the need to stop this horrid slaver from inflicting pain on someone. Even if that someone had just inflicted terrible pain on me. Thankfully one of the other Krektar intervened, "Farn you idiot! That's enough! He still needs to make the fertility drug, he can't if you make the weakling pass out."

Farn, the biggest Krektar, lowered the remote. He moved it towards me with an unpleasant grin and I had time to see that the dial was turned nearly all the way up. If he made me experience that, I had no doubt I'd pass out in seconds. I wouldn't hang in there for nearly a minute as the doctor had.

He was already struggling back to his feet, his creepy black eyes even looked shiny with unshed tears. When the mangy one, Frek gave him a shove he stumbled towards the panel near my side, right next to the wall with the creepy robotic arm. With shaking hands he worked the touch screen until with a hissing sound a panel opened below. "This should work," he said through bloodstained lips.

With a deep breath, he got his shaking hand under control and lifted a small metallic cylinder from the panel. "It'll only sting a little," he murmured and then he brought the thing down to my belly, unceremoniously rucking up my blouse and blazer to jam the thing into my tender skin. I hissed in shock but as promised it barely hurt at all.

"Done?" Demanded one of the Krektar males and when he nodded they started unstrapping me and without a backward glance dragged me out of the medical room. I struggled at first, terrified of wherever they were taking me. None of them had said what I was there for. Then Farn waved a meaty fist in my face holding the remote and I stopped fighting, allowing them to escort me through several metal hallways in various stages of dirty and disgusting.

I was relieved I was still wearing my uncomfortable but hella pretty black stilettos because the floor looked like it had been sprayed with blood in several places. *Oh crap, where were they taking me?* It was getting progressively worse too.

Another wave of fear swamped me and I felt my eyes fill with tears, I furiously fought against those. Crying was *not* going to help here. I hadn't cried when the slave doctor had performed surgery on me without anesthesia. I wasn't going to cry now. Though I really wanted to have a nervous breakdown.

A massive metal door barred our progress when we turned a corner and Farn, who was in the lead keyed in a series of symbols on the small screen next to it. I was close enough to easily see what he did and tried my hardest to memorize the ten-digit code (at least I assumed they were alien digits).

At my job at the bank, I generally coasted by, at least in the numbers department because I had a head for them. I remembered numbers as easily as I remembered my own name. I hated my job because of the human element; I should have just become an accountant.

My numbers quirk didn't help when I didn't actually

know which numbers I was remembering. Whatever translator tech the Doc had installed just went as far as translating what I heard, not what I saw, unfortunately.

The door slid open with a groaning sound, its mechanism clearly struggling. It became obvious why only when I was ushered through the door, two massive dents near eye height on the door disfigured the frame here.

Beyond the portal lay what could only be described as a wholly medieval-looking cellblock. No futuristic lights or panels, no white walls like in the medical area. Just gray metal walls and a ceiling that stretched far higher than could be properly illuminated. Not with the small yellowed and dirty floor lights that lined the hallway leading away between the two rows of cells.

The cells themselves consisted of metal walls on three sides and a barred front with no apparent door. The cell nearest to the door seemed empty and held only a small cot with a blanket and what appeared to be a metal bowl meant for waste. From its dirt-encrusted state, I could tell those were one of the main causes for the horrid stench that filled the place. It was clear none of these cells had been on the receiving end of a cleaning product in a long time.

"Are you sure about putting her in with the Beast, Farn?" The mangy whiny one asked from my left. "If he tears her to shreds, those hundred credits are a complete waste!" Those words did not fill me with confidence. Tear me to shreds? What the hell was the Beast? Which was clearly pronounced with a capital B.

"Oh shut it Frek," one of the others growled back, "It's not as if you wanted to pay your share of those credits anyway! The Beast is unique, we're going to get massively rich selling his offspring!" I could practically hear them salivating at those words and see the dollar signs in their freaky yellow eyes.

Except, it sounded like they were planning on using me as a broodmare for whatever creature this Beast was, just to get rich. Was that the fertility shot the doctor had given me? To help get me pregnant? The thought of some creepy alien using me and then these evil bastards taking the resulting offspring was awful. *God, these were terrifying thoughts.* I actually considered fighting them so they ended up killing me.

Then there were the occupants of the cells; they were enough to give me nightmares. While the first two cells had been empty, the next four sets held a prisoner each. As it was very dark in each cell some of the occupants were hard to make out, but a few came all the way to the front, to the bars, so I had a good view.

While the Krektar were ugly, they were bipedal and still appeared very humanoid, some of these prisoners barely resembled humans at all. I saw one male who was completely covered in a thick pelt and his head was shaped almost entirely like a fox; with mobile ears, coloring, and a thick tail included. As I passed his cell he licked at his snout and leered from an impressive height straight down my half-opened shirt. And he was clearly male because the scrap of cloth that covered his sex was barely adequate.

Another male had skin that was so closely resembling rock it was uncanny and his legs were shaped like a lion's legs, his face grotesque with fangs and tusks and horns. Huge leathery bat wings spread out behind his back with clawed tips. If gargoyles were real, this was exactly what one would look like.

I breathed a sigh of relief each time we continued past another cell with yet another terrifying creature. The end of the hallway ended in a slightly larger cell and I had a sinking feeling we were headed for that one. It was completely swathed in shadows, so I couldn't tell much about its occupant except for two glowing, emerald green eyes. That wouldn't be too terrifying on its own if it weren't for the fact that these eyes were at least seven feet off the ground. Whoever those eyes belonged to was humongous.

Now Farn paused, licking fat gray lips while he gave me a leer. "It occurs to me," he growled with annoyance. "That we should have sampled her ourselves before getting Doc to give her the fertility shot. After the Beast is done with her she'll be ruined..."

There was some groaning and grumbling from the other three Krektar. Who I noted stayed well out of range of the long-armed reach of any of the occupants of the cells. I wasn't sure if I was relieved or not that they now couldn't risk knocking me up themselves. Probably relieved; one rapist was better than five right?

"Rise and shine ugly!" Farn eventually yelled. He unhooked a long stick with metal prongs on one end from his belt and banged it against the bars of the largest cell at the end of the hall. "Show your ugly mug Beast, let your baby momma see what she's in for before we lock her in the dark with you."

I gulped in fear, my heart pounding and my palms sweaty as I awaited what was about to step into the meager light. *This was going to be bad, I knew it.* I was so desperately wishing I'd never gotten up that morning for work. *God, it probably wasn't anywhere close to the same day, was it?* I'd probably been in, what I was now realizing was a stasis pod, for a long time.

My attention was roughly snapped to the cell, away from my panicky, spiraling thoughts, when the cell's occupant stepped up in front of the bars and into the light. *Holy hell!* My breath stalled for a moment as I took him in. This guy truly was humongous, he was nearly eight feet tall.

The male before me was bipedal, with two arms and opposable thumbs but that was pretty much where the resemblance to a human ended. If you compared him to a crocodile on two feet you'd come closer, due to the green scales that covered him entirely.

Though his head was actually shaped more like that of a bull placed on top of a neck more like a triangle, his trapezius muscles were more like actual trapezoids than those of your average steroid-using gym rat. The reason for those huge muscles was obvious when you took in the bull horns that splayed wide and heavy from the sides of his head, they spanned easily three feet.

A blunted snout with a wide nose topped a maw filled with razor-sharp teeth, the canines long and pointed and deadly sharp. A thick gold ring pierced the nose and a row of glinting blades rose like a mohawk across his scalp to his back.

Fuck, crap, damn… I cursed in my head. His thighs were thicker around than my hips and that was saying something. Not to mention that those huge arms and feet were tipped with thick black claws and crap, but was that a spiked lizard's tail swaying behind him? *Oh god no, they wanted me to mate with this thing? Was it even sentient?*

I felt like utter crap for thinking that the next moment. There was a pain collar tightened around that huge neck, he wasn't here by choice any more than I was. Then I noted the one soft feature on his huge body, long ears, attached to his head just below the jutting horns, they were shaped sort of like a corn husk. Soft and mobile-looking they flicked once when my eyes landed on them, then drooped all the way down when I flinched at the sudden movement.

"On your knees!" Barked Farn, and he jabbed at the huge alien's thickly muscled belly with his pronged stick. He slid out of the way effortlessly, his emerald eyes fixated on my face. He'd moved with a dancer's grace despite his big body, and he hadn't even looked at the Krektar wielding a weapon at him through the bars.

The other Krektar were chiming in, all shrilly ordering for the Beast to get on his knees. He wasn't obeying though, a rebellious fire in his green eyes. When Farn raised the remote for his pain collar the huge male bared his mouth full of teeth and growled deep and low. Then on the sides of his arms, sharp looking blades fanned out and the blades growing out of his skull flicked upright, adding a good foot to his height.

The growl had clearly been directed at Farn but when I flinched back from the ferocious display those green orbs settled on me again. I had a feeling of keen and even calculated intelligence. The next moment, he focused on Farn and his pronged stick and in a move so fast I couldn't follow he'd yanked Farn right up against the bars. One fist had a hold of the stick and the other was wrapped around Farn's throat.

There was a moment of stunned silence from everyone

and then a cracking sound that would probably echo in my dreams for a long time to come. The Beast tossed Farn's body away from the cell with a contemptuous flick of his thick wrist; making it look effortless to throw the six-foot-tall Krektar right at my feet. He grinned then and for a sick moment, I wondered if he thought he'd just given me a gift.

The next moment the cellblock broke out in utter chaos. The other slaves imprisoned were hooting and yelling, stomping their feet in applause for the Beast's act. The other Krektar were yanking me back, shrieking in anger and fear, and then there was the Beast's roar of victory.

Until it ended when one of the Krektar, Frek, the scrawny one, found his pain remote and pressed the switch, dialing it all the way up. The Beast stared at my face the entire time his body convulsed from the pain, coursing through his nerves on the highest setting. Unlike the anthracite doctor who'd collapsed to his knees after a minute; the Beast stood his ground against that pain for a long time. A huge, immovable bulwark against oppression.

Eventually, his eyes rolled into the back of his head and he collapsed, his body hitting the metal floor with a thud so loud I felt the vibrations of it shake up through my own legs. *And they wanted me to mate with this creature?*

Frek was ordering the other two to push me into the cell, it seemed that despite Farn's death by a broken neck and his initial resistance to this plan, he was going ahead with it anyway. With a click of a button on one of their wristwatches, much like a smartwatch, several bars to the Beast's cell lowered into the ground.

"Get in!" yelled one of the two whose name I didn't know. I thought the two might actually be twins or clones, they looked so identically ugly. A wave from Frek's hand with the pain remote, just to warn me what they'd do if I didn't obey and I found myself squaring my shoulders, raising my chin, and stepping over the Beast's collapsed body into the cell. *Fake it till you make it right?*

The bars rose up behind me with a definitive snick.

CHAPTER 2

Ziame

Something was different today, everyone on the block knew it. There were restless pacing sounds coming from some of the cells and angry muttering coming from the winged Tarkan. We knew the day cycles by the way the lights in the hallway dimmed or flared and we filled our time with training for the arena in the ship's gym. Today our escort hadn't come, they'd left us to rot in the cells for the entire day cycle.

We'd docked, I had heard the changes in the engines as they'd idled down. We all had, but nobody had been taken from the cells for a fight, and they hadn't warned us that one was coming up. We were supposed to be headed for Xio for a round of gladiator matches, by my count that was still at least seven cycles out.

Then, after some hours the engines had roared back to life and we'd resumed our flight. Were we still headed for Xio? Was I doomed to fight again in seven cycles? I hadn't moved from my meditative pose yet but the restlessness was getting to me too. I found myself pacing my cell, slightly larger than that of the others, back and forth while my long tail swished behind me in frustration.

I needed to calm down, it wouldn't do to betray my ploy. As long as they thought I was a stupid mindless beast I knew they'd slip up around me again and again. Say things I shouldn't be hearing, maybe leave out a complex tool I shouldn't know how to use. I snorted in anger, and my fire-starter clicked in my throat. *Sure how long had I been keeping up that ruse?* Going on three years?

Flicking out my tongue I caught the scent before any of the others did. Female, tasty and sweet. *Damn it, what were the Krektar up to?* Had the slavers brought aboard a female for their own sick games or were they going to involve one of the males on the block? My hearts pounded in my chest; I hated seeing the suffering of the females in this universe.

When the other males caught the scent a few minutes later there was low talking among a few of them. Some angry growling from the Tarkan whose species was matriarchal like my own. *Yeah, I got it buddy. I wanted to rip and shred and kill to protect the unknown female too.*

The screaming started not much later, high and fierce and heartrending. They were hurting the female and it didn't sit well with any of us here. "Fuck," growled the Sune through his fanged maw, clutching at the bars with his clawed hands.

Behind him, I could see his plumed tail ripple and split, an anomaly even among his own race.

Pacing back and forth I growled in a low and angry rumble, and when the screaming halted every single male held his breath. Listening intently. Did she live? As she screamed again a second time, I figured she was getting translator tech installed without sedation, the barbaric assholes. How could they do this to a defenseless female?

Her voice gave out halfway through that second time and some of the males here flinched when that happened. "Did they kill her? Or did she pass out?" the Sune male growled in concerned frustration. None of us had an answer so nobody said anything.

The next while was hard, I wanted to know badly if she lived or not. In my three years as a slave owned by the shadowy crime lord Drameil, I had to learn how to steel my heart to these kinds of things. Yet, this time it tore at me far more than it should. She smelled too soft, too sweet, I told myself. She wasn't like a Lacerten female, armed with toxic venom and a fire-starter. This female smelled utterly defenseless, it wasn't right to hurt such a creature.

When the cellblock opened I retreated into the shadows, hiding from sight so I didn't have to mask my expressions. Relief bathed my features when I saw Farn and three other Krektar escort a human female inside. *She lived.* She walked proudly on shiny black stilts and she held her chin up high despite her fear. Her dark skin gleamed in the low light; she was the most beautiful creature I'd ever seen.

Tiny and delicate with curves that made me salivate and the hair! I couldn't believe the hair, it wasn't like any I'd ever seen before. So wild, so fierce, and curly it haloed around her delicate face like a cloud of the softest black, I wanted to sink my clawed hands in it so badly my palms itched. Shit, I was becoming a degenerate like these damn Krektar if I could have such lustful thoughts about a helpless human female like that. She couldn't fight back, she'd be so easy to dominate, to pin down.

They were headed right for my cell, passing the other males one after the other. The Krektar were debating her charms and *shit*, they were clearly about to throw her into my cell. They wanted me to rape and impregnate this female. *Stars no, never.* If there was ever a time to fight for freedom it was now when I had a female that needed my protection.

Farn was ordering me into the light so that she'd be able to see me. I didn't want to, because I knew I looked monstrous to her. She had clearly only just come from a stasis pod, she'd never seen aliens before and hadn't gotten used to all our variations. Seeing me would terrify her.

I had no choice, I had to get it over with, she'd see me eventually, and I needed to win her trust. I wanted her to see me and not fear me, to see me and see safety and protection. Surely my fearsome appearance would evoke that? Once I'd gained her trust?

Still, I found my ears drooping at the horror reflected on her face. It hurt, to have this female fear me, to find me appalling to look at. I was a Lacerten in his prime, I was strong and skilled and my horns had been the envy of my peers back home. I had a certain pride too, I was considered handsome before I'd left to explore the universe. Not out here though, as a gladiator, I was called an ugly beast and jeered at even as they applauded my deadly attributes.

I had to think fast now. Since they'd moved us from the

Caratoa, the slave ship they'd been transporting us on to Xio, to this rust bucket, there had been considerably fewer guards. We all knew the Caratoa had been attacked by pirates and the ship had been too damaged to continue despite winning the fight. This pirate ship we were now on, housed us in improvised cells. There were many weaknesses to exploit this cycle and I had far more to fight for now.

When Farn tried to strike me a second time I grabbed his shock stick, yanked him to my bars, and snapped his neck in a single move. There, now there was one less guard to deal with when I escaped. I threw his lifeless body down the hallway, dismayed to see it land right at the pretty female's stilt-clad feet.

I knew that they'd punish me with their pain collar, knew they'd hurt me until I'd pass out. Which was perfect, it would give the female a moment to acclimate to my presence while I wasn't so threatening. It would give us both time where the Krektar wouldn't expect me to get to it right away.

None of this was out of character either, I'd carefully cultivated this rebellious streak where I appeared too stupid to follow simple commands like kneeling. In my cell, I acted territorial and aggressive without fail. They wouldn't suspect a thing.

As the pain from the collar surged through my nerves, burning me from the inside out I found solace in holding the female's gaze. I felt sorry for her. Sorry, she had to witness my brutality, it wouldn't help us build trust. Sorry, she had suffered so much pain already, and sorry she'd been ripped from her home with no way to return.

Five minutes I endured, aware that any less and they'd suspect I wasn't really out. They were agonizing, slow minutes but I counted them down diligently. Then I let my eyes roll back and my muscles go slack so I thudded to the cell's unforgiving floor. As the pain collar switched off I kept my eyes closed. And though it was hard, I stayed slack on the floor even as the bars to my cell lowered and they sent the female inside. Escape now was foolhardy, even if I could endure the collar's pain, it did render me defenseless. I couldn't escape with it on.

Then it was time to wait, for the female to calm down and the Krektar to leave.

ᔕ

Abigail

They'd left me in the Beast's cell just like that. No orders, no warnings. Clearly, they figured that the Beast would take care of the rest of their evil plan without further prompting. Not for a while yet though, as he was passed out on the floor. At least they'd dragged Farn's body out of the cell block.

For long moments I contemplated the scalpel in my pocket, courtesy of the slave doctor. Was it smart to try and kill the Beast now? When he was out? Would that actually save me from the horrible fate of rape and forced pregnancy? Could I even do something so horrible? Even to a creature straight out of a nightmare who'd killed without remorse right in front of me?

"Get a grip, Abigail!" I ordered myself in a soft whisper and I palmed the blade, getting up to kneel on the dirty floor next to his huge head. How did I even kill a creature like this? Every single part of him looked deadly. In the extremely meager light at the front of the cell, I could see how every defined ridge and valley of muscle cast shadows on his barely clad body.

His chest was heavy with thick pectorals, his abs were well defined, and his arms roped and corded with muscle that even the thick, armor-like scales couldn't hide. Gold bars glinted from his nipples which at least indicated his species bore live young, not laid eggs like many lizards on Earth. The groin area was thankfully covered by a scrap of cloth, a loincloth, no way to see how sexually compatible we were.

Then my eyes flicked to the ears hanging slackly down in his repose from just below the truly impressive horns. They were as long as my hand palm and while they were covered with scales, these were so tiny as to make it look more like gently pebbled skin. Even in the dim light, I could tell that the base color on the outside was dark green with an intricate lattice of emerald lines crossing it, while the inside of the ears was the palest of green. They actually looked soft enough that I was tempted to touch them.

I was wrong, there was a single place on his body that didn't look deadly, his ears. They were heartrendingly pretty and endearing for a male his size. They made me remember the look in his eyes just before he killed Farn and the way he'd maintained eye contact all through the painful punishment of the collar.

Hadn't I thought he'd looked calculated and intelligent? I felt like he'd made some kind of pro and con list in his head before he'd decided on killing Farn. It hadn't been a beastly spur-of-the-moment thing, there was more in that huge head going on than just instinct. Though all the Krektar's crude joking about my encounter with him on the way to his cell had certainly made me expect a dumb killer.

Sentient then, I decided, so I found myself sinking to my heels, losing my ready tension as I lowered my knife-wielding hand to my side. So far I'd carefully kept it angled away from the light so I hopefully hadn't given it away to any guard who might be watching. I couldn't kill a sentient being like this. Maybe in a fight, maybe if he was trying to hurt me; but not while he was passed out on the ground.

That was probably incredibly stupid. I had no chance of fighting off this beast when he decided to come at me. Once the choice was made my brain brought up the look in his eyes as he'd convulsed in pain. Hadn't that been compassion? Why would he look at me like that when he was the one in pain? Surely I'd interpreted that wrong.

His breathing was still deep and slow, he hadn't moved a single muscle since he'd toppled to the metal floor like a falling tree. This was probably the only chance I'd ever have, so against all wisdom I reached out a single finger and gently stroked it down the side of one ear. My breath whispered out of me with a sigh, *wow that was even softer than it looked, how incongruous.*

Then his eyes flicked open and unerringly landed right on my face. I gasped, only just stifling a scream as it rose up in my throat. My entire body did the damned freeze thing again instead of choosing to flee or fight. It was like I was trapped in the deep emerald glow of that gaze.

A huffing sound came out of those huge, gold-ringed nostrils and I struggled to interpret it. Was that a laugh? He still hadn't moved otherwise, he was just looking at me. The suspense was killing me, I was struggling so hard to get my body to move, to back away. My thigh muscles were quivering from the strain.

"You may touch, tiny-female-of-the-big-hair," he rumbled at me softly, the corners of his mouth pulling up to reveal sharp fangs; though the expression clearly showed mirth. All the conflicting emotions, horror, and pain of the past hour seemed to bubble up inside of me. Everything seemed to misfire all at once in my brain. A laugh came out, crackling from my throat until bursting forth far too loudly in the deadly silence of the cellblock.

Tiny female? I had never ever in all my life been called tiny. Of amazonian proportions at six feet, I was taller than many a man I met. I'd given up on giving a crap about it years ago and happily wore my high heels and stilettos. Of course, compared to an eight-foot giant I would be tiny.

The hair though, yeah, I'd gotten that comment all my life. I was a melting pot of various ethnicities. My mother had been Nigerian, and my father was half-Italian and half-Vietnamese. *Yeah, I had enough mixed genes to not match with anything very much.* Except for the hair, which was as frizzy as it could get, definitely inherited that from my mother's Nigerian side.

Right now, it almost passed for an Afro because the hair products I normally applied had long since stopped working and my favorite hairband had broken the morning of my last day on earth. Hence why I had two thick rubber bands making a valiant attempt to restrain the whole mess.

During the entire time I was laughing hysterically, the Beast lay prone on his back on the floor, just watching me with what could only be described as a soft look in his luminous green eyes. When I quieted down he inquired softly, "Feel better?"

It sent me into another peel of giggles for some unfathomable reason; I was reacting like a complete lunatic. Until I suddenly felt something caress my bare ankle, then my laugh turned into a shriek. I looked down to find the tip of the Beast's tail had curled itself around my leg.

Scrambling backward across the dirty floor I stared at the thing with shock while the Beast rose to a sitting position, his tail sweeping back, letting me go without a fight. The tip was bare of spikes for about a good foot and I watched as it lazily curled through the air, coiling, and uncoiling, clearly very agile.

There were growling sounds in the air; they had to come from some of the other cells because the Beast was quiet as he watched me. When I made eye contact he nodded his huge head, horns tipping my way. "Easy female, I will not harm you," he murmured in a soothing voice.

I had a hard time believing that but he didn't move anymore; simply remained seated with his back against the bars. His huge legs were tucked close and his hands raised in a universal sign of surrender. I felt like my entire reality was turning upside down for like, at least the third time since I woke up. Was this guy not going to hurt me at all? Were the Krektar wrong about him?

When we'd sat like that for some time, without either of us moving, the Beast finally spoke again in a very low and rumbling voice. "I'm going to move towards the shadows, if I sit out in the light too long the Krektar will get suspicious."

He didn't move until I'd nodded at him from where I was pressed against the back wall. Unlike him, I was completely in the shadows but he clearly had no trouble seeing me. When he rolled to his feet slowly, I flinched and immediately

I saw his mobile ears flick back in response.

When he rose to his full height I felt my breath stall and fear make my heart pound. He was so freaking tall the tips of his horns actually brushed the ceiling. My lizard brain was fully in charge at that moment again, telling me to stay still, to not draw his attention any further. My mouth was dry in panic and it only increased as he moved into the shadows and sat down on the creaking cot. Now I couldn't see his face anymore, couldn't read him at all.

"They don't listen in on us, they only have cameras," the Beast said. "Bad ones at that. In the dark like this, they won't be able to tell what we're doing. Be at ease. I will not touch an unwilling female." His words reassured me, at least somewhat. I still didn't know if he was telling the truth or if he was just placating me so he could get close. When I thought about it, that seemed stupid, he probably outweighed me three times over, if he wanted me he could take me.

I nodded, incapable of vocalizing any of my racing thoughts. I was hard at work trying to figure out whether to trust this guy or not. He was certainly far more talkative than I expected him to be and I was almost starting to feel grateful for the painful translator surgery. At least I wasn't completely helpless, unable to understand what any of these aliens said.

Now that my mind was slowly calming, I became aware of the cold permeating the cellblock. This place wasn't getting heated like the rest of the ship and it was far cooler than my clothing could combat. Already my toes felt like clumps of ice in my pretty black stilettos.

"You are cold?" the horned male asked me when I had been sitting trembling and shaking against the wall for some time. I nodded, uncertain of what he was going to offer or say next. Did he think I'd willingly get close to him for the promise of heat?

After a short silence, I saw a shift of movement high up, his horns? Then there was creaking as he rose to his feet. "There is a blanket on the cot, I will move to the other side. You are safe." And then I heard his footsteps as he crossed in front of me from one part of the cell to the other. I waited a moment before I got up and found the cot by touch.

As I crawled onto it I found a warm spot, the area the Beast had been sitting on probably. I tucked the blanket tightly around me and then curled up on the spot. The bed smelled surprisingly nice, spicy, and sweet with a hint of male sweat that was more appealing than gross.

Though I tried to stay awake, to stay alert, the warmth and the smell and the exhaustion of all the hectic events since my waking from the stasis pod were too much for me. I sank into oblivion far quicker than I expected.

CHAPTER 3

Abigail

I woke up feeling warm and disoriented. Had I dreamed about a horrible alien abduction? I couldn't believe how crazy scary and detailed my dream had been. It had been so intense I still felt groggy and strange, and why was my bed so lumpy? Had I fallen asleep with my laptop in bed again?

Then the smells hit me and I instantly knew that I hadn't been dreaming; everything was real. I wasn't capable of imagining the combination of that fantastic male scent so close by and the overlaying smell of dirty toilets and too many sweaty unwashed men.

Blinking my eyes in the complete dark I struggled to make proper sense of where I was. Tears stung my eyes at how desperate my situation was. Lumpy cot, check. Ratty smelly blanket, check. Muscled, scaled shoulders as wide as a barn door to curl up against, check. Shit… the Beast.

For a moment I froze but then I realized that the huge male was sitting with his back to me on the floor, leaning up against the cot. One massive horn was tilted sideways into the mattress, supporting his head and the scary spines that formed a mohawk over his skull and down his back were completely flattened, harmless. He was what was smelling so nice and he was probably also the only reason I wasn't an Abigail-shaped Popsicle right now.

Then I noticed the tail, it was curved up onto the cot, curling around my body like a weird hug. It was actually long enough for the tip to reach the top of my shoulder. This guy was totally snuggling with me in his sleep, even though he'd done the super gentlemanly thing and sat on the floor next to me.

Greatly daring, I reached up to touch the scaly tip of his tail where it lay next to my cheek. Warm and dry; the scales felt smooth and soft. It was only about as thick as my thumb at the end but it thickened to about my wrist gradually a foot away from the tip. That's where the first of the spines started too.

I knew from the sound of his breathing that I'd woken him with my curious touch, but this time I was far less scared of him. It was oddly reassuring not to be alone in this cell right now. "What's your name?" I asked in a hushed whisper. I knew the Krektar called him the Beast, but somehow I very much doubted that was his real name.

There was a charged silence and then a soft sigh, "I have not been called by my true name for over three years. If you call me Ziame, I'd like that." Ziame was spoken in three syllables with the last ending almost on a purr that I would never be able to replicate. I tried nonetheless and was rewarded with a soft chuckle. "Thank you, what should I call you little female?"

"Abigail," I responded, "Are you going to do what they want? Get me pregnant?" I knew the second question was stupid to ask, how many choices did we have if they started enforcing it with a press on that pain switch? Torture me long enough and I knew I'd obey, likely Ziame would too.

"I won't let it come to that, don't worry Abigail, I have a plan," the huge male assured me, his body shifting so that he could look at me, though he never removed his tail curled around me. I was conflicted by wanting to not be touched at all because I wasn't sure what it meant to Ziame and needing his tail to feel warm.

"A plan to get us free?" I asked instead, focusing on the most pressing matter. His emerald eyes glowed catlike in the low light setting. Clearly, this guy had no trouble seeing in the gloomy dark, while I could barely make out his features at all. Maybe that was a blessing, as he'd looked so terrifying yesterday.

He nodded his huge head, "Free and safe." He paused as he seemed to think about what to say, "Our circumstances are ideal for it." Now my eyebrows shot up in surprise, "Excuse me, ideal? I wouldn't call getting abducted from my home ideal, buddy."

There was a low chuckle that was far too sexy for a beast like him, though that was hardly fair to think. Maybe the females of his species thought he was a total hottie. "Alright, not ideal for you. Though it was not the Krektar that took you, from what I overheard yesterday… It sounded like they bought a faulty stasis pod on the gamble you were still alive inside and their gamble paid off."

I shivered, I hadn't realized just how closely I'd brushed with death when I'd been unaware. I could have simply been gone, because of malfunctioning tech. I hadn't even the faintest idea when I'd been taken, how long I'd been out. Had years passed? Or days? Weeks?

"Okay, they gambled when they bought me, and then they thought they'd get rich quick if they managed to get me pregnant by you. Why?" That bothered me, of all the males locked in the cells here, they'd gone right for Ziame.

"I'm the only known, to them, Lacerten in the universe. I make Drameil, the male who owns all the slaves on this ship, a lot of money," he explained. When I gave him a curious look he expanded, "All the males in this cellblock are gladiators. They make us fight in matches all across the settled universe. Sometimes to the death. It is the highest form of entertainment for the elite."

Then he added with no certain amount of pride, "And I am undefeated. My species is simply too..." he seemed to need to think about a word here, "lethal naturally." Then he tapped a horn with one of his fingers and flared up the spiked row from the top of his skull all the way down his back. He had impeccable control though because none of the spikes on his tail flared where they lay against my body.

"You do look very lethal," I nodded, which was becoming comforting rather than alarming already. He snorted through his wide nostrils and then grinned, showing off fangs, I had pleased him by saying that. Truthfully, if I could have a guy like this on my side, there might be a ray of hope. He certainly looked up to the task of protecting me.

"And those are only the visible attributes. I have a venomous bite and I can breathe fire. Even without a weapon, I am never unarmed." He added, his teeth catching a little light and gleaming ivory in the dark. I suppressed a shiver at the sight, instinctively fearing that scary-looking maw.

Heck, this guy just said he breathed fire! That instantly made him more like a dragon than a lizard bull cross, that was so freaking awesome. Reaching out I tapped the scales on his wide chest with a finger, "And you always wear your armor too."

"Exactly!" he nodded, then darted a glance down the corridor. "Listen," he murmured, softer now and clearly a little more hurried. "Four days ago the ship we were transported on, the Caratoa, was attacked by pirates. The pirates lost but the Caratoa was too heavily damaged to keep flying. They transported us to the pirate ship. This ship." He pointed a finger at the metal flooring.

"They rushed to install these cells, or at least shore them up so they could house us here. But the crew is decimated. They are with less than half their number I believe. If ever we have a chance of fighting and winning, it is now."

I heard what he was saying. The fortuitous attack from the pirates had done half our work so to speak and then they'd locked them, us, in cells that were substandard. That did sound like far better odds than what he was probably used to.

What it came down to was probably whether the other gladiators were willing to fight with us. Though another problem occurred to me immediately. I fingered the slave collar that pressed tightly against my throat. "Yes," Ziame hissed, "As long as I wear the collar they can defeat me. I must find a way to get it off."

☙

Ziame

They took us from our cells after sparing us ten minutes to gobble down our water and food rations. Abigail had chewed listlessly on her tough bar and then after barely downing half of it, had pushed what remained my way. I'd eaten it without comment. Since our move to this ship they had been feeding us half rations and I could certainly do with the extra protein.

Leaving her in the cell, unprotected was hard but there was simply no choice. I had to tell myself they weren't going to touch her as they had given her the fertility shot and couldn't risk interfering and screwing up the intended product. Suppressing a growl at the thought of the filthy Krektar intending to sell my offspring, I focused on the poorly outfitted gym.

Two Krektar stood near the door, overseeing us working out on the various gym instruments. Some of us were at the weightlifting stations while others were paired up on the mats going hand-to-hand, sparring together. They wouldn't break out the wooden practice weapons until later in the day.

When they'd moved us from the well-outfitted Caratoa to this ship they hadn't bothered to bring much of the protective practice gear. Such as the mats that prevented nasty falls. The pirate ship had decent enough workout gear but the mats they did have were old and well-used. Already, I'd seen the Sune male, Kitan, make a fall that rolled him right off. He'd cradled his wrist but then cast a look at the Krektar and quickly hid the injury. To show weakness was a death sentence.

I considered the males as I lifted weights, the task almost on autopilot as I'd done it daily for years. Kitan and the Tarkan male, Sunder, had been in Drameil's stable less long than I had but I'd shared cells and the gym with them long enough to have some measure of their character.

Tarkans were from a matriarchal society, Sunder would never harm my Abigail so I knew I could count on him when it came down to it. I'd heard his discontent, heard his growls when he thought I was harming the female. Kitan was of like mind, though he was a reckless wild card in a fight, always doing the least expected. The male was solid though and neither of them had been born slaves, they were something before being forced to be gladiators. They might have skills that were useful outside of the initial fight.

For one, after we killed all the Krektar, we'd need someone to pilot this ship. I had some practice piloting Lacerten vessels but very little else. I didn't doubt I could learn to fly this ship but that would take some time, time we might very well not have. Not if the Krektar got off a distress call for example.

I didn't know the exact numbers of Krektar I was up against either. Still, as I contemplated my fellow gladiators and the problem, a plan was forming. Everything would hinge on getting my hands on a remote in the next few days, otherwise, I was going to risk grabbing one of the Krektar in the gym, and hope I could get to his before he could.

ෆ

Abigail

I hated it when four Krektar showed up, waving around their pain controllers as they escorted the males from the cell block. Ziame had warned me that he'd be gone during the day, they took all the males to the gym to practice for the upcoming fights. He didn't fight this time, though they ordered all the other males to kneel at the front of their cell except for him. Seemed to me like he'd won that particular fight previously.

As they led the males away I saw the Krektar in the back leer at me and I hurried to flinch back into the dark and cover myself with the blanket. I needed it to stay warm anyway but it wouldn't do for them to see I was still fully dressed and unharmed. They needed to think that Ziame had done a number on me.

I had noticed something odd though; only eight males leaving the cellblock. One cell near the middle hadn't been opened at all. Had I miscounted previously? Was that cell empty?

Curiosity had me get up, blanket clutched tightly around me and scalpel in my pocket in my hand underneath. I went to the front of the cell, stood in the light, and tried to look into the cell that hadn't been opened. There was nothing to see though, if there was someone in there they were all the way in the back where the light didn't reach.

"Hello? Someone still here?" I asked tentatively. Nothing stirred. Maybe that cell was empty after all, I couldn't remember if I'd seen someone in there last night. That walk through the cell block was a blur of monster-like creatures. Although as I'd seen them leave earlier I realized that some had looked quite humanoid after all. Maybe my fear last night had distorted things.

I shivered, trying to shake off my disquiet at being alone in the creepy cell block. Without Ziame here I felt distinctly vulnerable. He didn't think they'd come for me, or that they'd harm me but I still felt like a Krektar could show up at any point and drag me out of here.

Just as I was ready to turn back to the cot and curl up on it I saw something move. That cell, there was something in there after all. I nearly shrieked with fright when a monstrous face moved into the light, only just managing to stifle the sound in my hand.

A beast, a real beast was in there. Not some creature like the gargoyle or the fox-like man, not anything like Ziame. This creature was on four legs, with sleek black fur and a face with a maw full of razor-sharp teeth. Eyes like red coals glowed at me for a moment and then the creature turned and padded back into the darkness.

Shit! Holy crap! That creature was freaky, it moved far too fluidly, it was just uncanny. It looked like it would eat me up in a single bite! No wonder they'd left that one in there. It wasn't sentient, at least that seemed extremely unlikely. The collar around its neck indicated that it too was probably here for the same reason those other males were.

Couldn't let that one loose in a gym though, it was probably far less capable of understanding commands. They probably barely controlled it at all with that collar. That was just a wild animal, plain and simple.

I was still contemplating the freaky beast a long time later when a Krektar showed up, carrying a large haunch of thawing meat. It tossed it through the bars into the beast's cell without comment and then wiped his bloody hands on his pants as he came my way.

From the cell, I could hear the sound of the creature eating, bone-crunching sickeningly. Though I was more concerned with the lewd look the Krektar gave me. He was getting closer and I had the feeling I wasn't going to like what was about to happen next.

"You're up, sweetheart," he said and he tapped at the small screen strapped to his wrist. The bars to Ziame's cell slid down into the floor at the command and the Krektar gestured for me to get out. "What are you going to do with me?" I asked, I didn't feel like getting out and into the range of those sandpaper-skinned, grabby hands.

He smiled evilly at me, displaying a row of greenish and black teeth that probably would benefit from a good mouth scrubbing. They stole me from Earth and thrust me into some sci-fi nightmare with spaceships and translator tech, and yet the bad guys still didn't understand dental hygiene? This guy was truly disgusting, far more so than any of the males I'd seen leaving the cell block earlier.

Since I hadn't moved from my spot on the cot, frozen in place, he moved his hand to his belt where the pain controller to my collar dangled. "Hurry up! Or don't..." he smirked and I slid to my feet, not in the least interested in getting to feel the effects of that pain collar for myself. Maybe that was cowardly but on the other hand, I reasoned, just sitting in this cell wasn't going to provide me with very many chances for escape.

I left the blanket on the cot and the scalpel folded inside

it. I was worried that if I took it with me it would be discovered and I had no chance of fighting off the muscled Krektar without help. Maybe, when Ziame came back to the cell tonight, I could use the scalpel to get off his collar.

So unarmed, I stepped out of the cell, straightening my wrinkled power suit as I did so and holding my chin up high. With my high heels and with my height, I was just as tall as the Krektar escorting me and I could tell from the way he eyed me up and down as we walked that this intrigued him.

The halls we traversed were as dirty and creepy as before and now that I knew this was previously a pirate ship it made more sense. Probably it wasn't just dirty and neglected-looking, those smears on the walls might very well be remains of this ship's previous owners.

Luckily the Krektar took me to the medical room where I'd woken up without another word and without touching me. Inside was the anthracite male who'd given me my translator tech but otherwise, the room was empty.

He nodded once at me and then focused his creepy, completely black eyes on my Krektar escort. "Thank you for bringing her Thonklad, wait outside, this is going to make you squeamish." The guard, Thonklad wasn't one from the bunch the night before. He appraised me for a second and then looked at the doctor before he nodded.

"I'm right outside, if I hear anything I don't like I'm pressing the control for *both* your collars!" he threateningly pointed at the remote on his belt again and then he turned and strode out of the medical room; the door sliding shut behind him. Taking with him a nasty smell, so it wasn't the dirty smell of the cell block lingering on me.

The doctor gave a long sigh and then gestured around at

the immaculate place, which was a far cry from what I'd seen of the rest of the ship. "Welcome to the medbay aboard the Caratoa 2.0. I am Doctor Surgeon Lukalyn Nerizana, sadly currently owned by the crimelord Drameil."

Oh, introductions… Huh, here he had me freaking out about what kind of procedure he was going to put me through that would make the Krektar squeamish. I actually darted my eyes at the door for a moment to make sure the guard was really gone before I raised a questioning eyebrow at the Doc. "Really? Introductions? After you threaten me with scary procedures?"

He had just been gesturing for me to sit down on the medical cot but immediately dropped his hand, shoulders slumping beneath the immaculate white coat. "Right, I see now how that came across. My apologies."

Then his creepy eyes darted to the door as well, "Thing is, Thonklad is on the young side for a Krektar to be serving Drameil, only thirteen year cycles. I'm told his previous commission was on a merchant's vessel that saw very little action. He's still very squeamish about a lot of things."

"Thirteen! He's just a kid?" I demanded, shocked since he'd appeared fully grown like all the others. I had to try and adjust my view of the guard that had just left, were they all so young? Or were their life spans just shorter?

Now the doctor shook his head, "No, fully grown I assure you. Krektar life cycles are fairly short, thirty cycles thereabouts. Just a little less experienced than the others aboard the vessel." He picked up a hand device of some kind, it looked a little like one of those price tag scanners in a supermarket. "Now, please sit on the cot so I can make sure you're in good health, I promise no injections and no scary procedures."

I looked at him for a while longer, making sure he was sincere, then shrugged and sat down where he indicated. It was silent for a while as he ran the scanner over me and checked his readings. Eventually, it occurred to me the doctor might well know far more about the ship than Ziame and I could find out from our damn cell or the gym.

"So… Can you say your name again? I think I missed it… I'm Abigail by the way." *Okay, as far as olive branches go this one sucked but that didn't seem to matter to the Doc.* His face broke out in a smile, he was so pretty when he did that it took my breath away just for a moment. Only the scary eyes marred that picture. Geez, whoever gave him those killer cheekbones sure knew what they were doing.

"Abigail, thank you. My name is Doctor Surgeon Lukalyn Nerizana." He beamed some more and I actually found the straight white teeth and the super human features covered in that oddly glittering anthracite skin a little disconcerting. Maybe Ziame had already grown on me because somehow his fanged grin was more reassuring than the good doctor's smile.

"That's a mouthful…" I heard myself say, *rude*!

But the doctor just nodded, "Oh, I heard humans like to shorten names, it's a sign of friendship! Would you like to shorten my name?" My god this guy was upbeat and cheerful, it really was a little strange and he clearly thought that if I shortened his name that meant we were friends.

"How about Luka?" I offered and he nodded his head, black silky hair swinging forward over his shoulder. "And call me Abby alright?" There was no harm in letting him think we were friends, and I hardly minded if anyone called me

Abby, most people did.

"Abby! I'm most grateful. I truly hope you can forgive me for yesterday's barbaric surgery." I wasn't certain if I could do that but he'd brought it up several times, once right after the surgery even. Thinking about it some more I remembered how he'd given me the scalpel and warned me, hadn't he? I eyed the collar on his neck, he was a slave too. They'd even demonstrated the use of the collar on him, without a single warning. He wasn't holding that against me.

"Forget about it," I said with a wave of my hand. "You had no choice did you?" Nobody had much choice about anything aboard this ship, it was hard to wrap my head around it. About the cruelty, these Krektar, and the slave owner so carelessly showed.

His eyes closed at my words and he sighed, "Correct. I have been conscripted into service as of sixty-seven months ago." He tapped the collar around his neck. "I will do all I can to make you comfortable, to keep you healthy Abby. Please, did the Beast harm you? The scans are good but that doesn't say everything..." His eyes darted to my belly, or was that my crotch? "He's not so bad as the Krektar make him out to be… I'm sure he's not…"

He sounded so worried that I shrugged, "It was alright Luka, I'm okay."

His expression immediately brightened, "Okay, that's good." He sat down on a rolling chair then, "I'll keep you here as long as possible. It's warmer here than in the cells and I worried you'd get too cold without the Beast keeping you warm." Oh… He really just wanted to make sure I was okay, he'd been worried and he'd clearly had enough power to get me out of the cell for some time. I was grateful to be in a warm room instead of that freezing cell.

"Can you tell me how many Krektar are on board? How many guards?" I asked. I could immediately tell I'd surprised him but then he tilted his head a little sideways and nodded. "You are thinking of escaping?"

I shrugged, "I gotta try Luka." He held his breath a long moment, those freaky eyes fastened to my face. "Alright, I'll tell you what I can."

CHAPTER 4

Ziame

Abigail was waiting for me on the cot when we returned from the gym; I was infinitely relieved to see her. Which meant I felt free to act out a little; having been compliant nearly the entire day. I appraised the four Krektar escorting my fellow gladiators and me back to our cells. *Ah, that was good to see, the newest recruit was among them, he'd probably fumble when I made a ruckus.*

I weighed my options for a quick moment. Would they do something to Abigail if I hurt another guard? They hadn't last time and I knew they truly thought I was practically a mindless beast, incapable of speech. When the damn crime lord and his flunkies had managed to capture me, I'd made such a spectacle fighting they hadn't realized what I really was. They hadn't even bothered to try and equip me with translator-tech the way they did most other slaves. A slave who understood your orders was quicker to obey after all.

Thankfully, I had my own tech installed and it was far superior to the tech that was standard in the universe. My translator implants were neural and worked for the written as well as the spoken word, they adapted and learned new languages on the fly. The tech they had brutally put in my Abigail only worked for the languages in their database and sometimes faultily at that. Not that there was much better out here, to get something as good as what I had, we'd have to return to Lacerten somehow, impossible.

I kept track of the four guards and the remaining gladiators. I figured I could maybe frighten the nearby two enough for them to back into some of the others, they'd possibly do the work for me without putting Abigail at risk of reprisal.

I waited till the last moment when the two in the cells nearest to me were only just stepping in and I was nearest my own cell. Then I swiveled my head, snorted in a deep gust of air, and let my lungs do their trick, oxygenating that air hard on the exhale. My fire-starter clicked in my throat as a warning and then the exhale caught fire.

My aim was perfect. The cone of flame sprayed right between the two Krektar at my back and they hastily jumped out of the way. Just as I'd hoped their frantic leap landed them right into the arms of Sunder and the wiry, scrawny Geramor of the blue fur.

I knew just how vicious Geramor was, of all the gladiators I was the least certain of his morality. In this, he came through exactly as I'd hoped. The opportunity, in the heat of the moment, was too good for him not to keep his many fangs in his mouth.

While I backed away and into my cell, blocking Abigail from sight and possible reprisal. Geramor opened his huge, double-hinged mouth and ripped out the throat of the Krektar who'd stumbled into his cell.

Sunder was far more practical. In that one flash of a moment where I'd sprayed the hallway with my fire, I'd seen his face. He grabbed the Krektar nearest him, not even letting chance have a say in whether his victim ended up in his cell. Just like I'd done with Farn last night, he snapped his victim's neck with an air of economy and practice; tossing the body out of his cell and bowling it into the remaining two panicking guards.

He sat down on his knees the next moment, placing his hands on his horned head in surrender. Making it at once clear he did not intend to harm the other guards. Smart because that meant the scrambling Uru, the senior of the two guards, snapped his bars closed but didn't engage his pain collar.

My cell closed as well but Geramor was doused on the highest setting by the pain collar. Incredibly, the carnivorous male had started eating the Krektar he'd caught and he didn't immediately stop eating either. *Yuck.*

It took two minutes on that high setting before he lost consciousness and thudded hard to the floor of his cell. During that time all of us were utterly quiet, hearing only his agonized moans and the thrashing of his heels on the floor when he collapsed.

What was going on behind me was far more interesting

though. I knew I'd scared Abigail with the eruption of violence and she was clearly horrified to see Geramor suffer, to see him try and eat the guard he killed too if I could hazard a guess.

Instead of staying behind my broad back, the female had looked, of course she had. Instead of backing away, shuddering in fear or repulsion, she had placed her small hands on my scaled back; anchoring herself to me. Almost, as if my presence gave her comfort but I didn't dare hope that was already the case.

"Did he just start eating the guard?" Abigail asked me in a hushed whisper, shock evident in every single syllable. I rolled my shoulders, "Yes, Geramor's species, the Hoxiam are extremely carnivorous, they need vast amounts of meat and he's not getting nearly enough." I didn't add that their species tended to live off the thrill of the kill and the hunt just as much and enjoyed eating all kinds of sentient races. They were spacefaring but banned from all ports and planets, except when enslaved, of course.

As soon as Geramor passed out Uru ordered Thonklad to pull the body of their fellow guard out of the cell. It obviously wouldn't do to let the Hoxiam male have access to any of the guard's gear or to let him continue gorging himself on his flesh. They knew as well as I that on large quantities of fresh meat a Hoxiam nearly doubled in size. It was only done for certain types of fights, which meant that Geramor was always half-starved. Sad and horrible if his preferred food wasn't sentient races.

Once the body was out, Uru closed the cell and the two Krektar worked to dispose of the bodies with little fanfare. They were not the type to get sentimental so I wouldn't be surprised if those two bodies simply went out of the airlock without another word said. At least it was good to see that Thonklad definitely seemed a little green around the gills when handling the corpse mutilated by Geramor.

They returned throwing rations into our cells and then, on their heels Frek came. "Shit, he's come for the punishment," I murmured at Abigail who'd taken the bars and sat down with them on the cot. I hadn't wanted to start eating yet so she had the two meant for me as well.

"He's the type that gets off on hurting those bigger than him, isn't he?" Abigail scoffed in a hushed whisper. I fought a grin at her description, *oh yeah that was spot on*. I knew his type well, they always set the pain collar higher than warranted, and always kicked a little extra when you were already down. Weak little bullies.

"Curl under the blanket, stay out of sight," I said as a warning in low tones. I really didn't want Frek to set his sights on her. Bully or not, he wouldn't hesitate to harm my female if he thought he could.

"Thought to stage a little rebellion did you Beast?" the wart-faced Krektar demanded as he stepped in front of my cell. I hadn't backed away into the dark, hoping that playing target would make him less likely to focus on Abigail. At his words I cocked my head, scraping my horns against the bars of the cell and then shaking my head a little as if I got confused when one horn got stuck for a brief moment.

Frek laughed uproariously, pointing at me and then looking at the other Krektar, "Look at the dumb beast. He was probably just attempting to swat a fly!" The three Krektar laughed, but I saw the look in the older Uru's eyes, he was thinking hard. *Shit... That wouldn't do.*

Then Frek turned to gaze into the dark shadows where my cot was, I knew he couldn't see Abigail but that didn't seem to matter. "Too bad you're not pregnant yet. For you! You'll have to let that beast between your legs again! I only wish I could see that, hear your pretty screams."

I smelled Abigail's fear, she was shaking on the cot, trying to stay quiet and hidden. Stepping into Frek's line of sight I growled, flaring up my spines and the blades on my arms in a territorial display. He was close enough that if I breathed fire he'd be burned to a crisp, the clicking of my fire-starter would give me away though. It was too slow a weapon.

Frek didn't raise his hand, there was little warning, but the pain flared to life through my collar. It roared through me at the highest setting and I groaned in surprise and instinctively advanced toward him. Bashing my hard skull and thick horns against the bars of my cell.

Behind me Abigail screamed, "Ziame! No stop it! Don't hurt him!" she was behind me then, grabbing my arm at the elbow and trying to pull me away from the bars. I had no control of my muscles though, it was all I could do to remain standing. That damn coward Frek had engaged the control on the highest setting. It was far harder to resist this pain, to stay conscious but for Abigail, I tried.

Somehow, my hands unlocked from the bars and I staggered back a step, pulled backward by my female's meager weight. Another staggering step while I groaned, focusing hate-filled eyes on the gleeful Frek. Then I sank to my knees and forced myself to turn to stone.

"Don't want us to hurt your big stud do you, tasty human?" Frek taunted and from the corner of my blurry eyes, I saw Abigail's pretty face pinched with fear and worry.

She wasn't even looking at the Krektar anymore. She just looked at me, then I saw the moisture pooling in her beautiful brown eyes and felt like a total heel. I caused that. If I hadn't instigated this round of violence she wouldn't be crying now.

A huge exhale rolled out of me, angled down and I saw wisps of fire curl into the air. The pain coursing through me had made me lose control of my fire-starter and it clicked in my throat. I couldn't risk burning my Abigail so I fought hard to turn my head away from her. Locking eyes instead with Sunder kneeling in his cell patiently. The older male knew he was next but his look conveyed understanding, sympathy, and support; at least I liked to think it did.

I held myself strong as long as I could stand it and then, just like the evening before, faked my fall from consciousness. Opting to throw myself to the side Abigail was standing on so that I fell on top of her. Though I caught my weight on my palms and made sure Abigail didn't hit the metal floor hard, instead her head landed on my curled arm. Then I pinned her, sort of.

I hoped that if I was on top of her like this, apparently out of it, they wouldn't want to have to bother dragging me off her to get to her. I could shield her from them, even while they thought I was out of it. And of course, when I faked my fall, to Abigail it was utterly real and she screamed in fear and possibly a little pain.

"Not exactly what I had in mind when I said I wanted to watch," Frek jeered and Abigail moaned and feebly struggled to get her hands up and push me off. I didn't let her but I shifted my weight a little more so I wasn't crushing her as much. When I did she stilled and I felt her turn her head into my throat, the sensation of her breath on my scales blocked partially by the collar but pleasant all the same.

As my head was angled just right to look into Sunder's cell I slid my nictitating membranes closed over my eyes and then opened my eyelids a little so I could see what was going on without giving myself away. Frek had turned to stand in front of the Tarkan male's cell and was appraising the male, who sat stone-still, clearly patiently waiting for his punishment.

"You at least know exactly what you did," Frek said. "Doesn't make you less stupid. You do realize you are slated for death your coming match?" Sunder rolled his shoulders, his wings pressed tightly to his back. "I know, so what do I have to lose?"

That was right, Sunder was one of the oldest males on the cell block. He had seen nearly ten years of gladiatorial combat and lived to teach the newer males about it. In the gym, he was the one setting the exercises for us, responsible for pairing us up, and training us to be our best. But Sunder, as far as being out on the sands, was definitely past his best-by-date. Rumor was, he'd done something to anger Drameil, enough to get set up in a death match he couldn't win. He'd made himself valuable as our trainer but not valuable enough.

Frek contemplated the male a little longer and then shrugged, "Fair enough. But I could kill you now or you can die in another seven days. What do you prefer?" I nearly laughed at that, if I hadn't had Abigail I knew what I would choose.

Sunder surprised me, "You can't kill me now." His deep baritone was concise and certain. "If you do, you'll lose your master a lot of credits. He has bet against me on that fight, if I don't show up he'll lose out. You can't afford to incur his wrath Frek or you'll find yourself in my position next."

Frek let out an angry howl and jabbed the pain control on Sunder's collar. The older male fell to his hands and knees but stoically bore the pain the way I had. He bared his fangs at Frek but didn't make a sound. Not until he thudded to the floor several minutes later, head awkwardly falling against the wall. Thankfully, that male had skin like stone and a skull made for headbutting like mine, he could handle that kind of knock without injury.

The Krektar said nothing as they left the cellblock, though Frek gave a sharp warning look to each of the males awake. As the door slid closed behind them with a deafening thud Kitan let out a long loud sigh and then he tssked, "Was all that worth it?"

The males erupted into conversation, aware that none of their words were recorded. "Yes! Of course! There are so few of them now, we need to whittle them down!" one said and another scoffed. "We'll never get out of our pain collars, they'll always have the upper hand."

There was loud angry growling from the mind-broken beast that drowned out everything for a moment and then the conversation flared up again. The males were hard at work trying to recall how many guards were left, an admirable attempt. I desperately needed to know this information myself. We had to know the odds we were up against. I wouldn't risk Abigail without it.

CHAPTER 5

Abigail

He was hurt, again! I couldn't stand seeing that awful Frek hurting the males in the cells like this, especially not Ziame. I knew I did something stupid when I tried to defend him, drawing attention to the fact that I was not scared of him. That I cared.

When he started to collapse I had only a short moment to panic and then he was on top of me and we fell to the hard floor like a ton of bricks. I expected that to hurt a lot, I practically saw my life flashing before my eyes. Ziame had to outweigh me at least three times, *I was going to get crushed!* That is if he didn't poke an eye out with one of his horns or spikes.

Somehow my head landed softly on his arm and I managed to get my hands between us to push at him. He didn't budge of course, far too heavy. I barely heard Frek when he said something, instead, I focused on how I felt. Was I really in one piece? With nary a bruise on me? Oh wait, had Ziame just shifted his weight?

Ziame's arm cradled my head, my face was in his throat and his legs were on the outsides of mine. One long arm stretched out up along my head, his bicep brushing my hair. He wasn't that heavy at all, I should be crushed but I most definitely wasn't.

As Frek moved his attention to the male looking like a gargoyle I tucked my face close to Ziame's throat. He smelled so damn good, spicy and familiar. Already the scent symbolized safety to me and I was certain that if I could bottle this and sell it on Earth as male cologne I'd make a fortune. It was so damn good, especially pressed up close like this.

I didn't miss the fact that finally, after a long interminable day of shivering from the cold on that cot, I was at last toasty warm. His scales were warm where I touched them and with his entire body engulfing mine it was like I had my own personal heated blanket. Maybe a little heavier than I liked but not all that uncomfortable.

The Krektar finally left the cellblock and I took a chance and whispered very softly against Ziame's throat. "Are you awake?" There was no way he was this light, he was propping himself up somehow, but he was doing an admirable job making it look like he'd passed out.

My suspicion was confirmed when I felt his muscles tense

beneath my fingers a little, "I am, my Abigail." His whisper was even softer than mine and it sent a little shiver down my spine, goosebumps breaking out where his breath coasted across my skin.

"Did you fake fainting?" I poked at him and now there was the softest little growl.

"I did not! I faked losing consciousness." I laughed quietly, of course, males the universe over were sensitive about such things. I asked him if he could get up because I wasn't exactly happy about lying on the dirty floor.

There was a brief pause and I listened to the background noise of the males in the cell block arguing about the effectiveness of killing the guards the way Ziame and Sunder had done. "Not yet little one, it needs to look real." Oh well, I wasn't really complaining. I happened to like being warm at last.

"Are you alright?" I asked him, aware he'd just suffered through a hell of a lot of pain. "Why did you do that?" I didn't want him to take risks like this. He was my only protection in here, if he got himself killed I didn't know what would happen to me.

"Fine, I am tough. Don't worry." He shifted his head a little so that his face was angled more my way, it was now pressed into my wild mess of curls. I heard him sniff and I inwardly cringed; without a shower for god knows how long, I doubted I smelled as nice as he did. "We need to whittle down as many guards as we can before we try to escape. That is why."

Oh, that made sense, he'd caused the death of three guards since I'd gotten here. That took the number down considerably. It was, it seemed, the same thing the other males were now debating. "Twelve left then, plus two confined to bed rest who are still injured from the fight with the pirates."

Ziame didn't immediately respond to my statement, but I could feel the tension radiating from his body. "How do you know?" he asked and I felt a stab of hurt at his suspicious tone.

"I asked the doctor, who's a slave too by the way." I recalled the eager way he'd shared what he'd known with me, how his creepy eyes had gleamed with excitement. I was certain the doctor was on our side when we staged our escape. *If we even got the chance.*

"The doctor touched you again!" now he sounded angry and it finally made him move. He flowed to his feet and let out an angry roaring sound and shook his head so that one of his horns rattled against the bars to his side. I remained frozen on the floor and he leaned in suddenly, picked me up with his huge hands, and then he retreated with me into the darkness surrounding our cot.

The cell block had descended into silence at his outburst so everyone could hear me when I said indignantly. "Don't manhandle me you big jerk! The Doc only checked if I wasn't hurt, like I said he's as much a slave as any of us here!"

Ziame huffed loudly as if he didn't believe me, "He put translators in your ears without sedation! It's barbaric!"

"He didn't have a choice!" I yelled back, sitting up on my knees on the cot and planting my hands on my hips as I squared off with him in the dark. I was filled with a surge of adrenaline, but I wasn't scared at all. It was a little exhilarating.

"He talks?" someone asked and then someone else said,

"Go female!" "Did you know he could talk?" "What arcane magic is this?" demanded a last voice and then Ziame let out another loud roar that had me clamping my hands over my ears and silenced all the gladiators.

"I could always talk," he huffed in a pissed-off voice and I heard something click and then two thin tendrils of fire curled away from his face. Lightening up his angry countenance for a moment. He cast me a narrow-eyed look and then started pacing in the dark. His tail swished into the light at the front of the cell with each pass, with the spikes flared up.

Then there was a loud sigh as if he was surrendering to the inevitable. "I was just biding my time," was the explanation to the stunned gladiators who'd all gathered at the front of their cells to catch a glimpse of him.

"How is this possible?" asked a male standing two cells over, it was the one who closely resembled a fox on two legs. "You've been faking a lack of intellect all this time?" he sounded incredulous and slightly offended.

"Hey, watch your tone!" I snapped, offended on Ziame's behalf that this male had thought so little of him. There was a wicked grin from the fox and a round of chuckles from the other males. Heat scaled my face, I was unsure how to respond to any of this, but I sure knew I didn't like that they'd thought so lowly of him.

"Abigail," Ziame said with a sigh, "That is what I wanted him to think. It means I did it well." I knew that, didn't mean I liked it.

The gargoyle male had rolled to his feet and flared out his huge bat-like wings. "I had a feeling, I met one of your kind once," he said in that heavy baritone. His voice sounded much like rock grinding together. "You have a plan to get your female out?"

My eyebrows shot up. I'd heard how Ziame had been referring to me as his and I'd noticed some of the other males say it but it hadn't sunk in until this statement. Then to think that that gargoyle male was talking of escape solely for me as if that was the primary concern… That was strange and oddly flattering.

"I have a plan," Ziame said simply. Then his green gaze shot to the immobile body of the blue-haired, cannibal creature. *No wait,* I suppose it wasn't cannibalism as they weren't the same species. It just seemed really wrong as the Krektar were sentient, even if they were cruel and horrible slavers.

When Ziame focused on me in the semi gloom I could only see the outline of his huge, horned head and the glow of his green eyes. "Abigail found out the number of Krektar left." When he didn't elaborate I realized he wanted me to share the numbers myself. I rose to my feet, feeling better when I stood at my full height and then some on my stilettos.

"Twelve, and two injured confined to bed rest," I said and then I added, "The doctor can remove the collars, circumventing the tamper-proofing but it takes time. Time we won't have when escaping." There was some muttering and one voice claiming that made things impossible.

Ziame shushed them all just by making a soft growling noise, instantly all eyes came back to him, drawing the attention of the other males. "We get our hands on one pain controller and one of us can keep countermanding their orders, we can keep fighting."

That sounded like a worst-case plan, risking getting disabled in a fight over and over? But this seemed to cheer up the fox-like male, "That sounds doable. Let's all think about it. We can surprise the two guards in the gym easily."

There was some more talk then, but Ziame didn't mingle more. Instead, he returned to where I was standing next to the cot. "Take off your stilts and sit down, we should eat and then sleep." I gaped at him in the dark. "Stilts?" then I had to laugh as I touched the long pointed heel on one of my stilettos. Stilts was apt I suppose.

We ate in silence, sitting knee-to-knee on the cot, with the blanket tucked tightly around me. It was so cold in here that I only seemed to feel warm when Ziame was touching me. Last night, that thought had been pretty terrifying but I'd gotten used to him, I kind of liked him. He was really good at fooling everyone that he was a dumb beast, but he was smart and sensitive to my moods, and the kindest person I'd ever met.

The ration bar I was chewing on was hard and tasteless and I struggled to chew the stuff without taking sips of water in between bites, from the single water bottle they had supplied. In contrast, Ziame devoured his bars in two big gulps. Thankfully, this stuff was high protein, dense and heavy, and incredibly filling so only three bites in I felt full.

As I laid down for sleep the big green-scaled male started to gently tuck me in and I almost asked him to join me just so I could snuggle up against his warmth. The cot was far too narrow for the two of us though, in fact, it was probably too narrow for him by himself. I wouldn't be surprised if his feet dangled over the edge if he laid down.

Instead, I happily curled against his shoulders for heat

when he sat down with his back against the edge just like I'd woken up this morning. When I moved to touch him that way he seemed to take that as an invitation to raise his tail and curl it around me, adding warmth and safety.

It wasn't until my fingers grazed the scalpel I'd tucked between the mattress and the cot that I even remembered I had it. I only hesitated a moment, then I asked Ziame softly, so the other gladiators wouldn't overhear. "The doctor gave me a scalpel that first night, do you think we can use that to take off our collars?"

Ziame stiffened in surprise immediately, "You have a small blade?" He turned in his spot, keeping his tail tucked around me but facing me, his arms braced on the small bed. "Let me see it, please," he asked, keeping his voice low and quiet as well.

I didn't see much more in this dark than the soft glitter of his eyes and the vague outline of his big body but when I pulled out the scalpel I had the feeling he saw perfectly well. "Yes, this is small and mobile enough, we can pry open the lid and disrupt the insides. That should work. Now, to figure out how to get around the tamper-proofing."

Oh, of course, it wasn't that simple. If there was no tamper-proofing he'd probably have pried the thing open by now with one of those retractable claws of his. "What kind of thing are we looking for?" I asked, hoping he knew a workaround.

After a silence, he said, "I've heard the collar shocks the person tampering with it. So I suppose any kind of shielding would work." While I'd always been great at numbers, physics was a whole other cup of tea. I had never aced those classes, unfortunately.

When he talked about shielding I thought of medieval wooden or metal shields first before I tried to wrap my head around what kind of thing he could really mean. "Shielding as in something to keep your hands from touching the collar or the knife?"

A soft chuckle and then Ziame bend his big head closer to mine, I felt his warm breath caress my face and my body responded by raising goosebumps from the back of my neck all the way to my wrists. "I mean something to shield your hand from touching the knife. A thick piece of cloth, a glove, or something. Or maybe something to wrap around the handle of the knife itself."

Oh… wait *my* hand? "You mean I have to disable your collar?" I knew absolutely nothing about mechanics, I wouldn't be any good at such a thing! I was breaking out in a cold sweat just thinking about it.

"Yes, I'll get hit with the highest setting of pain regardless of what we do… I can't be the one wielding the knife." I mulled that over for some time in silence but I found that I had to begrudgingly admit that it was the only way. He'd proven several times that he could handle the pain, he was clearly willing to go through it. The problem was, it felt like a lot to carry, knowing I was the one pressing the button so to speak, made things very different. I didn't want to hurt him but if he was willing then I had to put on my big girl panties and just do it.

With that issue resolved I finally remember something that might actually be useful. "Rubber is good for shielding isn't it?" I asked breathily, still trying to be super quiet so no one on the block could overhear us. I had the feeling that Ziame didn't trust all of the gladiators to be on board, to so openly talk of rebelling made him uneasy. I understood that.

"Rubber is perfect, but I checked the soles of your stilts, they're wood and leather," he said as if he'd thought this through already. "And none of the fabrics of your clothing are pliable enough or thick enough to work well without some thorough shredding." He left unsaid that he obviously wore next to nothing, sacrificing his loincloth for it wasn't going to be helpful.

Reaching up into my tangled curls I struggled with the two thick rubber bands I'd used, what seemed like a lifetime ago, to restrain the whole mess. Once I got one free and held it up triumphantly he smiled back and I actually saw the glitter of his fangs in the dark. "Perfect!" I struggled to free the other while he went to work diligently wrapping the handle of the scalpel with the first. Adding the second one for good measure.

Once done, he tucked the blade into my hand and folded his fingers around my shaking fist. "I'll guide the knife to the right spot, after that you'll have to work fast to pry the panel free. Once open just cut any wires you see and that should do it."

Panic seized hold of me for a brief moment, "You mean right now? In the dark? I can't see a thing!" I hissed at him. But he was nodding, I could see the way his big horns bobbed up and down.

"Yes now and in the dark, or the Krektar will see and come in here guns blazing." *Okay live in the moment, I can do this!* I sat up on the edge of the cot, braced one palm on Ziame's brawny shoulder, and let him guide my other hand with the knife to the band around his throat. Pry off the lid and cut the wires. *Easy peasy lemon squeezy.* I just had to do it in the dark, where I couldn't see the seam of the panel *or* the wires I was supposed to cut.

"Ready Abigail?" Ziame asked in a husky whisper.

"No… But let's get this over with," I squeaked back at him. He pressed the scalpel with my hand against something hard and then there was a hissing sound as the doorway to the cell block slid open and raised voices as four Krektar barged in.

Shocked I slid back on the cot and hurriedly tried to hide the knife. Ziame was calm as he turned around to face the front of the cell, his broad back offering protection from view. Had they overheard us? Were they about to bust us for trying to escape? For tampering? I was scared enough that my heart was pounding in my throat.

Then I saw what the Krektar were dragging in with them; a slight figure with long blonde hair. They were arguing about touching her, not in a rapey way but in the 'I don't want to touch this filthy thing' kind of way.

The first two cells in the hallway were empty and they'd opened one of those and were escorting the small figure inside it. The light caught the figure just right and I saw a frightened, tear-streaked human face beneath that tangle of blonde locks. *Shit! A human woman!* Her body was small and slender except for her belly which was bloated. *Holy crap!* A pregnant woman at that.

They dumped her inside carelessly and retreated as if they got burned; the cell slammed shut practically on their heels. The Krektar looked around suspiciously at the rest of us in our cells but nobody said anything, we just watched. I watched with bated breath, I couldn't believe my eyes. Another *human* girl!

As soon as our guards left I turned to Ziame, "See that! A human woman! We've got to help!" I couldn't see his expression in the dark, the lights in the hallway had dimmed the moment the guards left. I imagined he looked both worried and skeptical. Knowing him he'd want to help but what could we do from in here?

I got up and walked to the front of our cell, pressing myself against the bars. "Hello? Can you hear me? I'm Abigail, I'm from Earth, New York to be precise! Are you okay?" There was a long silence and it surprised me that none of the other gladiators were pitching in. They'd seemed super interested when I'd been escorted down the hallway.

Eventually, there were shuffling sounds and a tremulous female voice spoke, "The city or the state?" I couldn't help but laugh, it was just too nice to hear a fellow human, even if that meant I wasn't the only one in dire circumstances. "The city of course!"

"God… I can't believe this is real," the woman spoke sadly. "Tell me your favorite comfort food please, something an alien wouldn't know..." I rolled my eyes as if naming a dish would prove anything. But I could understand her need to be reassured, maybe to even hear some familiar words.

So I said, "New York Cheesecake, Matzo ball soup, Belgium chocolate, clam chowder, pizza!" Just saying the words made me hungry, I seriously doubted I'd ever eat any of those things again. The woman must have had the same thoughts because I heard her crying. She didn't say anything for a long time, so eventually, I started talking to her.

"I know it's not a comfort, you've been stolen from your home, same as me. But it's going to be alright, I'll keep you safe. There are more allies here than you know." I didn't know what else to say, didn't know how to help the poor woman and she just kept crying.

The others on the cell block said nothing either, probably they understood far better than I did the realities we were facing. Maybe they didn't want to offer her any false hope but I really wanted, no needed, to believe in Ziame's escape attempt. I didn't think I could face it if that didn't work out.

My big green cellmate came up behind me at some point and curled the blanket around my shaking shoulders. "Come lay down, get warm again. There is nothing you can do right now." I knew he meant well, knew he was right even but it still made me angry. I hated being helpless, hated having all my choices taken from me, and hated being unable to comfort a crying woman because we were locked up like animals.

Stiff shoulders and balled fists didn't deter Ziame though. He picked me up bridal style as if I weighed absolutely nothing, instead of being a six-foot-tall woman. He placed me on his lap as he sat down on the cot and curled me tightly into his arms, rocking me. It wasn't until I'd calmed down a little that I realized I'd been crying too. Damn it! I was stronger than this! I was!

CHAPTER 6

Ziame

I hated seeing my Abigail cry. She had been so brave and strong from the moment we met, fighting back. But hearing her fellow human cry, talking about home, it had reminded her of all she lost. I held her tightly in my arms, offering her solace and warmth and feeling grateful that at least she was letting me give her this.

When she'd exhausted herself she finally fell asleep and I was grateful for that too, it was good to find a moment of peace in dreams. I didn't even mind that now I was still stuck with the hated pain collar another day; the appearance of the new human had to change our plans. We needed to make absolutely certain that she too was safe while we fought and defeated the guards.

I debated what to do for some time, my conscience wanted me to tuck Abigail into bed and sit down next to her like I had the previous night. I liked holding her close to me too much though, I'd been touched starved for three years and I was soaking up the weight and warmth of her body against mine like a plant soaking up water in a desert.

It wasn't just that though, it was Abigail, she smelled so good and she was so beautiful with her dark brown skin and wild black curls. Then there was that brave clever mind of hers, she hadn't given up once and I didn't count now either. I was certain that come morning she'd bounce right back, ready to figure a way out of this new predicament too.

In the end, I lay down with her on the cot, it was too small for both of us side by side; the damn cot was too small for me, period. With my feet hanging over the end and my right horn scraping against the wall I could lie on my back with Abigail curled up on my chest, tucked close with my arms and my tail.

Like that it was easy to fall asleep and when I woke up that next morning with her still right there, tucked up all warm and cozy, that was easy too. I wanted to bask in that moment, in her presence just a little longer but I couldn't wait to see her open those pretty brown eyes which were tilted just a tad, making them look sharp and clever.

When she woke, she froze for a brief moment, her eyes blinking in the dark and I was reminded of the fact that her eyes needed far more light to see in these settings than I did. Then she inhaled deeply and burrowed her cold nose against my throat. "Ziame," she sighed, and then she added a little more sternly. "I usually don't sleep with a guy before he's bought me dinner."

I didn't know what buying her dinner had to do with it precisely but I caught her meaning just fine and hope soared through my chest. I didn't care what I sounded like at all when I asked with a parched mouth, "You mean to say you'd be amenable to such things if I did?" I know I didn't say it out loud, how monstrous I looked compared to her but I was certain she understood.

Her body shifted a little and I stifled a groan at the feel of her sweet curves sliding against the hard planes of my body. "I..." she said and then her shoulders straightened and I knew I was going to get total honesty, I braced myself for rejection.

"Yes, I think I'd like that," she said. I stared at her, shocked, surprised, and suddenly oddly happy. I hadn't been happy in three long years so it was a very strange feeling to experience. "Really?" I asked and I could hear how husky and shocked my voice sounded, no doubt she heard it too.

One delicate hand reached up to pat the side of my face, "Yes. Really, I'd like to get to know you better. Once we're not stuck in a cell together and are free to make our own choices." I reveled in the soft stroke of her fingers on my scales and then realized my cheeks were hurting, probably because I wasn't used to smiling anymore.

Still, honesty bade me tell her of our differences. "You must know that my mouth… It's far different from those soft tempting lips of yours. My species, we can't kiss the way humans do." Her fingers froze for a moment on my face and I could practically hear her thinking, then said fingers slid down my jaw.

I didn't have a sharp snout the way the Sune had but it

was more snout than flat-faced like a human regardless. My blunt snout was tipped with a wide nose that had been pierced with a gold ring. That was a common thing among my species but my owner perverted it, enjoying hooking a chain to it and parading me around on a lead like I was a dumb beast of burden.

Now, Abigail's delicate fingers trailed across that nose and touched the ring and it wasn't until I heard the shallow intake of her breath that I focused on her instead of my own thoughts. Flicking out my tongue I tasted the air, her pheromones, and I realized her scent told me many things; none of them bad. She did want me, she was attracted, and touching my face which was so very different from hers wasn't putting her off.

"I think we can work around that as long as that's the biggest issue," she murmured, sounding thoughtful. Despite her darker skin, I could easily detect the heat rising to her cheeks. "Uh… I mean, if the other parts line up alright that is..."

Ah, she wanted to know if my cock would fit. This at least I could confidently answer with a solid yes. "Do not worry, I am much like a human male in that regard, we will fit," then I groaned at the imagery those thoughts provoked. We were getting ahead of ourselves, I was at least. She'd agreed to try to explore a relationship, not share pleasure immediately after we got out. She might not want to at all once she was free and had more choices.

The thought of her getting to know one of the other males in the cell block, picking one of them to share her bed with. It had me fight back an angry and possessive growl. I didn't think I could handle seeing her with another male.

Abigail was still blushing but she was leaning up towards my face, one hand reaching up to curl around the base of one of my horns. "That's good to know," she said and then she pressed her lips to my cheek. "Seriously Ziame, you smell so damn good. How do you do it? I must stink to high heaven after several days without a shower. But you..."

I preened at her compliment but then reassured her, "You smell fantastic to me. Honestly, Abigail. Besides, they let us shower after our training sessions at the gym." She groaned and thumped her small fist on my pec, "That's not fair!"

The lights came on in the hallway then and Abigail stiffened, "Shit! We're idiots, we should have worked on your collar and instead, we were flirting!" Maybe she had a point, but I couldn't regret a single bit of that conversation.

Nuzzling my nose against the side of her face I inhaled her precious scent and enjoyed the softness of her curls against my scales. "We need to change our plans, the other female is unprotected right now. We have to make sure she isn't harmed."

She sighed and tilted her head so I could nuzzle at her throat. "Oh, okay, I'll try to talk to her today." Then she had to let go of my horn so we could get up and receive our breakfast from the belligerent-looking Thonklad. I let my hands slide down her back slowly when we got up, wanting to linger in the closeness. I didn't release my tail from where it wrapped around her ankle until I was taken from the cell with the other gladiators for another day at the gym.

ꟹ

Abigail

Oh my god, I'd slept in Ziame's arms and I'd slept like a baby! Even after he'd left I was still sort of floating where I sat huddled on the cot in my blanket; it still smelled like him. Waking up on top of his warm, firm body was far more comfortable than it should be considering that he was covered in firm scales.

Never mind the fact that his tail had wrapped around one of my legs and a single hand of his spanned the entire width of my back. I had felt coddled, protected, and positively tiny. I had never in all my previous relationships felt like that. My last ex had literally broken up with me because I was too manly and independent.

I was still blushing from our conversation too, had I really decided I wanted to try and date this guy? This alien who told me his mouth was too different for kissing? But who claimed his cock was alright. Shit, was I willing to go there? Not right now but at some point? Have sex with him? The heat curling between my legs told me I absolutely was and I was a little shocked. I had never thought someone so alien would do it for me but I guess it did. Maybe it was because Ziame was so damn nice, I certainly felt like he deserved to have a good time after all he'd been through, and how he'd protected me so far.

Forcing myself to get rid of these thoughts I tried to focus on what really mattered right now, getting out of here. Getting that other woman to talk to me, hear her story, reassure her somehow. I should be focusing on that, and on staying warm obviously because I was already missing my big guy a lot.

I remembered the way his tail had stayed curled around my leg until the very last moment fondly. I'd never been one of those clingy girls who wanted to constantly sit next to or touch their partner, wherever they went. But that tail, damn that was just so pleasant, to feel connected like that. *Sigh, okay get your mind on track girl!* I had to help that other lady.

Standing I curled the blanket tightly around my shoulders for warmth and headed to the bars so I could possibly see the newest arrival. She hadn't made a peep yet all morning though I knew the guard had thrown food into her cell just like with everyone else.

"Hey, can we talk? Are you alright?" I asked, feeling a little stupid, maybe she was sleeping. It was only about thirty feet between us, the other cells were much smaller than Ziame's cell after all. Still, it felt a little like I was yelling across a street, hoping an acquaintance heard me.

After a few seconds, there was a shuffling sound and then a human face pressed up against the bars. She was similarly tucked into her blanket but she didn't seem to be shaking from the cold the way I was, a relief to be sure. I had worried she was freezing in there, she didn't have her own personal space heater during the night.

Her pregnant belly looked terribly misshapen and out of place but maybe that was because she was so small and thin; it was disproportionate. Most women got that rounded glow to their face, this poor girl was sallow and thin. Like she hadn't been eating enough.

"Hi," she said softly when we'd stared at each other for a moment. Her pale pink face was tear-streaked, her eyes red-rimmed and bloodshot. The long blonde hair lay limply against her thin shoulders.

"Hi, are you hurt?" I asked, feeling concerned for the poor woman. She was clearly not in any way, shape, or form okay.

She shrugged, "No, just pregnant." There was a scathing laugh, "Which I didn't even know until I woke up on a freaking alien spaceship last night!" Then she clapped her hands over her mouth looking horrified she'd spoken, her face turning red.

I was a little horrified myself, "Are you saying you were flat as a pancake one moment and woke up with a beach ball in your belly? Shit, that's rough." I was a little horrified about how graphically I'd just described that, but the young woman didn't seem to mind.

The woman nodded her blonde head with a pained look on her face. "I'm Tori by the way… I know you said your name is Abigail?" She was clutching tightly at her blanket, her eyes darting from my face to drop down at my feet, almost as if she was scared to hold eye contact.

"Tori, nice to meet you, I guess." I said and snorted, "Under the circumstances, that is. You can call me Abby." Then I checked to make sure the door to the cell block was still firmly closed before adding, "I know all those guys in the other cells look utterly terrifying but some of them aren't so bad. Ziame is working on a plan to get us out. It'll be soon, so you just need to hang on in there a little longer."

She sighed and rolled her shoulders in, making herself small but bravely nodded her head, "Okay..." We talked for some time, and I learned she'd just scored her first big role on Broadway which was awesome. Not so awesome that she was missing all that. I learned that she was a New Yorker just like me and from a big Italian family which was probably worried out of their mind right now, the last made her cry and effectively ended the conversation for a while.

I was almost relieved to see Thonklad show up with a haunch of meat for the beast in the cell in the middle. Sadly for Tori, it was across the hallway so she had a perfect view of the creature as it lunged for the meat and started noisily devouring. I heard her chanting, "Oh god! Oh god! Oh god!"

Then Thonklad approached my cell and told me to get out and follow him as I had another doctor's appointment. As we passed the cell I could see only the huge outline of the big creature and its glowing red eyes in the dark.

Though my Krektar guard wanted to hurry me past Tori's cell I halted and met the woman's tear-stained face. "What about her? Doesn't Doc want to see her too?" I looked at the wart-covered face of my jailer and caught a guilty look just in time. "Oh, he did want to see her but you don't want to is that it? How's your boss going to react when he finds out you jeopardized the health of the product?"

At my sharp words, the Krektar growled but it petered out into a sulky kind of sound while he gestured angrily at Tori in her cell. "She's got some kind of disease that could be deadly to my species. I ain't touching her!" My wide eyes darted to Tori who looked pale and frightened but she gave a little shrug that told me this was news to her too.

"Well, you don't need to touch her, and if anything that makes it even more important for Doc to see her doesn't it? The sooner he cures her and all that..." Thonklad looked like he'd swallowed a lemon, or maybe a whole bucket of them because his textured gray throat worked hard a few times, his tusks quivering.

"Fine!" he threw his hands in the air but then opened Tori's cell with a click of a button and anxiously scooted back. I on the other hand gently wove my arm through hers and guided her with us through the disgusting hallways to the medical bay. I noticed just how tiny this woman was compared to me, especially since I was still in my favorite pair of stilettos. She came up to my armpit and that was it, I had forgotten how much I felt like a giant on earth. It should feel unpleasant but it was somehow oddly comforting too.

"Are you sure about this?" Tori whispered softly at me and I gave her a firm nod but eyed Thonklad just in front of us. Was he going to be waiting outside like yesterday or was he going to be watching us the whole time?

I shouldn't have worried, the moment we stepped out of the dirty hallway and into the immaculate medical room our guard nodded at the Doc, pointed at the pain controller for our collars, and then turned on his heel. As the door slid closed I waved, "Hey there Luka."

While my casual greeting made the handsome but scary-eyed doctor beam a smile my way it caused Tori to squeak and then hide behind my back. Those scary eyes of his made quite the impact, I couldn't blame her. I'd caught the Doc's pained look though, he didn't like it when his patients were scared of him.

"Are you both alright? Not too cold?" he asked while he gestured for us to take a seat side by side on the medical cot. The two of us had to help Tori up onto it, and once she was sitting she was looking even paler than before.

I shrugged, "Ziame kept me warm." When my words made him frown in confusion I added, "The Beast."

That had Tori gasp in fright, "Your cellmate is called that?" Her eyes were huge in her thin face as she stared at me. I had the strong urge to wrap my arms around her shoulder and offer her more comfort, so I did.

"That's a good thing," I told the young woman, "It means he can protect us," I explained, she could see that, couldn't she? Even if Ziame wasn't such a softy underneath all that scaly armor, I would have tried to get him on my side.

Luka had taken his hand scanner to check on both of us and now he nodded, "He's good to you? I'm glad. I was so worried for you that first night." His had twitched once around the scanner as if he was wrestling with some strong emotions.

"Thanks," I said and I meant it, this guy was a marshmallow. It was the scary eyes that made him look terrifying but really, once you got over that part I realized he was nothing but kind. In fact, I would bet that he absolutely would take the doctor's oath to do no harm seriously.

"You're both healthy, the baby too," he said when he'd finished looking at his scans. This time I frowned and cast a look at Tori but she was gazing at her bloated belly with a look of fear and revulsion, absolutely not the picture of a happy mother-to-be.

"What about the disease Tori has that's harmful to the Krektar?" I asked and gestured at the girl in question and then flapped my hand at the door behind which Thonklad stood. Was that what was making her look so thin and unhealthy? And though I didn't want to think it, should I be keeping my distance so I didn't catch it myself?

Luka raised his creepy eyes to my face and gave me a cheeky grin, "I made it up. I figured they'd find that believable for a few days and that would buy her some time."

Tori looked up and stared at Luka for a moment in stunned surprise. "You lied to them to keep me safe?" I wasn't surprised that he had, but this revelation seemed to finally ease some of Tori's fear of the doctor.

Luka beamed back at her with his widest smile and nodded, "Of course. I don't want to hurt any of you. I convinced them putting translators in without anesthetic would be harmful to the baby and they don't want to lose it so..."

Huh, lucky for her. I still remembered what a bitch that had been and from Luka's guilty look at me I knew he remembered that too. I shrugged, "Alright, how long can you keep us here where it's warm? Is it possible to take a shower?"

CHAPTER 7

Ziame

"We cannot risk the new woman, she's pregnant," Sunder told me under his breath while the two of us sparred on the mats furthest from our Krektar guard. I knew that, that's exactly what I'd told Abigail that morning but unease ate at me, we needed to move fast. The closer we got to Xio, the smaller our window of opportunity became.

"Tonight, I'll get my collar off," I said to Sunder as softly as I could so not even any of our fellow gladiators would hear. Out of everyone here, I knew I could trust him the most, Sunder was solid and dependable, he was a survivor, but he also had honor. "Tomorrow during our workout, I'll take care of our guards. Then we move."

His slate-gray eyes appraised me for a moment as we circled each other and he gave me a curt nod. "I'll wait for your signal brother," he said, tranquil patience in his expression that told me he was capable of containing himself until then. After that neither of us spoke, focusing on the mock fight, keeping up the appearances for the time being.

A while later I was settling on a bench to lift weights when the Sune male, Kitan came over to spot me. I figured this was to talk because the male had on this journey so far generally paired up with the extremely morose Xurtal Pu'il. Pu'il was sparring with one of the others though so it could also be chance.

Especially when Kitan just silently helped me adjust weights and carefully watched my form as I did my reps. For the longest time, he said nothing at all though it wasn't uncommon for the males to joke and talk about previous fights when they had breath to spare. Of course, I'd never been part of these conversations because I'd carefully kept up the appearance I couldn't talk in anything but grunts and had no translator.

The truth was that no translator in the galaxy had the Lacerten tongue uploaded to their database. If I wanted to make myself understood out here I spoke one of the known languages, typically the most often spoken traders common.

Eventually, Kitan said what he came here to say, his growly voice pitched low so only I would hear. "You are the sneakiest male I have had the good fortune to meet. Whatever you have planned, you can count on both Pu'il and me to back you up. Give us a sign and we'll fight." Ah, so he and his friend had spoken about this.

"You know Pu'il well enough to be sure? I didn't realize you two knew each other," I asked. Only Sunder, Kitan, and Geramor had previously been housed in cells near enough for me to know them. Pu'il, like the rest, had only come aboard for this particular flight to Xio. They had been picked up at another location.

"Yes, he and I were in the same stable for a year, we've trained together often," the Sune male simply said, not in the least offended that I'd asked. That was good enough for me, I couldn't be picky after all and the goal was to free everyone by the end of this revolt.

I needed to know where I stood with these two a little more though. Sunder I knew had a death sentence hanging over his head; he had nothing to lose fighting this fight, and his matriarchal society made him more inclined to want to protect the two females aboard. Kitan and Pu'il were both strong fighters, it was likely they'd come out victorious in their upcoming matches on Xio.

"This could end in death for any one of us, you understand that right?" I asked the male, eyeing the Krektar at the door to make sure they weren't paying attention to us. The guard was propped against the wall, fidgeting with his gun, and clearly bored, *good.* Kitan shrugged, rippling his fur-covered shoulders in a fluid move while he kept one hand out beneath the bar as I lifted. "At least we'd die free." I couldn't argue with that.

"Thank you, I'll be counting on you," I offered, happy to know that these males were backing me up in my crazy plan to break free. "What we need," I added, deciding to unburden just a little now that I had the chance, "Is someone who can fly this damn ship once we've killed the Krektar."

Kitan chuckled and sent me a wicked grin, "I'm your male then brother. Aren't you in luck?" He flexed his free arm, wiggling his fingers. A spark rose in his golden eyes that I was familiar with, the desire to fly, the true drive of someone who'd sought out space to be free. I was pretty sure I'd once had that same spark in my eye when I'd been granted permission to leave Lacerten and explore the universe.

"You're a pilot?" I asked, a little incredulous because I hadn't pegged the always restless and active Sune male to be able to sit in a pilot's chair long enough to fly a ship with any skill. He was always in motion and flying a spaceship could become boring very quickly.

"It's soothing," he said, then with a glint in his eyes added, "And fun!" The Krektar were looking at us now, probably because Kitan had spoken just a tad too loud, and I wasn't supposed to be a conversationalist. "Oops," the male said with a gleeful chuckle and then he abandoned me to join up with Pu'il and start a practice fight on the mats. I was left to angrily glare at the weights and snort tendrils of fire in the Krektar's direction, which served to make them back away.

The rest of the day I spent carefully going around each of the other males, making it a point to work out with them or next to them so I could check that each was on board with this rebellion. I even spoke with Geramor who'd given my Abigail the creeps when he'd started eating the Krektar guard he'd killed.

All day I was anxious to return to my cell and see Abigail again. Every hour I was away from her I worried she was being harmed while I wasn't there. The Doc wouldn't conclude she was pregnant obviously, but maybe that Krektar Frek would get impatient. He was a sniveling bully after all and with Farn dead he was in charge of this ship.

ᔕ

Abigail

I was actually sort of happy after Thonklad returned Tori and me to our cells. It was still cold but the Doc had scrounged up some old jumpsuits from somewhere to wear over our clothing. It was big on me but Tori was positively drowning in the thing, which meant her pregnant belly actually fit. It helped immensely to stay warm.

On top of that, the Doc had delivered; both Tori and I had gotten to shower and wash our hair. I felt like a new person almost, *rebellion bring it on!* And cuddles with Ziame too, now I didn't need to feel self-conscious about my scent; even though he'd assured me I smelled good to him.

I was pacing in the cell, heels clicking along when the doors finally opened and the men were escorted back inside. This time there weren't four guards but eight, they clearly weren't taking any chances this time around. I hoped that meant Ziame wasn't going to try and kill any of them tonight, I wasn't sure if I could handle seeing that a third time.

Ziame in the light in the hallway looked magnificent to me, huge even compared to most of the other males. His green-scaled skin wasn't just latticed with emerald on his ears, I could see that the same pattern also curved over his flanks and on the outsides of his arms. His wide horns made the hallway seem small and as he had lightly flared out the row of knife-like spikes along his head and spine; he looked super intimidating.

He looked nothing like a human man, that was for sure but I couldn't help but feel this primal tingle of appreciation. That creature could protect me and provide for me, it ticked all the right boxes and on top of that, he was kind and sweet. *What more could a girl want?* The glowing green of his eyes seemed even brighter when he caught my look and I just knew he was happy to see me. Even though he didn't change his expression all that much he seemed brighter at that moment.

The transfer into the cells went smoothly, even if I could see how nervous the Krektar were, their hands hovering over their pain switch buttons. They expected trouble. I knew Ziame wanted to whittle down the number of guards though, so I wasn't sure if this was a good thing or a bad thing. I was relieved anyway, I hated how Ziame had paid in pain each time.

Once we'd sat down and eaten our terrible ration bars I carefully told him about my day and inquired about his. That felt so very domestic and normal that it was a little jarring. Ziame brought up the fact that he'd spoken with every male and they were all on board with our plan, which almost seemed too good to be true. Maybe not that surprising though, living as a gladiator had to be really hard. Then he said, "Tomorrow. We'll do it tomorrow during the time we are at the gym." His worried eyes focused on me, "I just worry about leaving you here in the cell alone. I do not like that part."

"I think it's likely that Tori and I will be with the doctor for some portion of the morning, try to time it then? We'll be safer there I think." The thought made me nervous too but it was better to be out of the cells and with Luka who could help fight if it came down to it. In the med bay, we'd have access to sedatives and more scalpels.

"That is a good plan, I will try to time the uprising for that moment." The first day I'd spent about an hour in the medical bay, today had been double that, because now Tori was there. That gave him a fairly large window. At least, unless the doctor changed the schedule and brought us to his medical room in the afternoon instead.

When the lights went out we huddled next to each other on the cot and Ziame pulled the scalpel out of its hiding place. "It's time," he whispered and he wrapped my fingers around the blade and brought it up to his throat. "You can do this Abigail."

I couldn't see anything now but I knew it needed to be done so I climbed to my knees. Before I could change my mind I leaned up and tugged on one of his big horns to bring his head closer. Then I nuzzled his cheek and pressed a kiss to the side of his fanged mouth. "For luck," I said and I could feel the corner of that mouth turn up in a smile. Then he leaned in and nuzzled the side of my face, rubbing a little more firmly against my temple. "For luck," he whispered back.

We settled into position and I tried not to hesitate as I let Ziame help me slide the knife into the seam on the control box of his collar. As soon as it was in between the casing and the lid I could sense how Ziame stiffened, his hand around mine twitched. *Shit! He was already getting shocked!*

I forced myself to focus as I pressed the blade a little deeper, leaning with my other hand on his shoulder for leverage. The lid popped off with a clack and fell to the bed between our knees. I didn't wait, just swished the small blade through the inside of the casing, twisting it around for good measure until I felt Ziame lose his tension. "Well done!" he whispered huskily, but I could hear a faint tremble in his tone. That had hurt, a lot and he hadn't made a sound.

Taking the blade from my suddenly nerveless fingers he placed it on the floor at our side and then tucked me into his arms and stroked my back. His tail curled around to twirl around one ankle, anchoring me to him in every way possible. "It's over, you did great little female," he said, and I soaked in his reassurance.

"I'm so glad that worked!" I murmured, "I don't know what I'd have done if I had to try that a second time. I'm so sorry that hurt you," I told him with heartfelt sincerity. I hated these collars, I was terrified of the one around my own neck. I couldn't believe how strong he was to bear the pain that thing inflicted so calmly.

Ziame just rocked me for a while and at some point I realized that it was comforting to him too, to hold me close. He was rubbing his head on top of mine, in my curls, a contented sigh leaving his lungs. "I'd gladly go through that again and again if it meant freedom little one."

Of course, this was about freedom and he'd been a slave far longer than I had. Three days didn't compare to three years at all. Knowing that I clutched him a little tighter for a long moment, returning his back stroking with some petting of my own.

Then the silence was suddenly pierced by a voice, high

and sweet it soared in song. I didn't know what song Tori was singing but the lyrics were poignant, singing of freedom and hopes and dreams. She hadn't been kidding when she said she was a singer, the girl had talent.

When the song was finished there was a hushed sound to the cellblock and then the sound of stomping feet. I realized that Ziame too was stomping a foot on the metal flooring, alien applause it seemed. I half expected Tori to pick up another song but when the alien applause died down I heard her soft sobbing and I just knew she was crying for all she'd lost.

Eventually, Ziame told me to lie down on the cot, he still needed to do some work on the collar to make sure it looked like it still functioned. For warmth he sat with his back against the edge, tail curled around my body. I listened to the quiet sounds of his tinkering, occasionally we whispered about our lives pre-kidnapping.

I learned that the Lacerten, his species, were highly advanced but very peace-loving and they had hidden their planet from the rest of the universe. Sometimes males like him went out to explore the universe but generally, nobody left home. He'd been taken on his exploration mission and they'd never discovered his cloaked and hidden ship, instead assuming he was a barbaric creature incapable of speech.

He told me with a laugh that was probably because they'd caught him while he'd been sunbathing naked. He claimed it was because he'd taken a swim in a pretty lake he'd found on the planet he'd been researching, there was an amused twinkle in his green eyes that I could see even in the dark. If they'd seen him wearing clothes they'd probably have known he was sentient but as he'd been naked… I kinda could see why they had assumed that he was not.

In return, I told him about my boring life as a bank teller on earth and how my parents had had me late in life and they'd both already died of old age. I had no close family left to yearn to return to, not like poor Tori. I surmised I was probably taken right after work from the parking lot, mostly because of the rubber bands and the way I was dressed.

At some point I fell asleep because I woke curled up on Ziame's chest again, his big hands covering my back, and his tail curled around a leg. Sighing I snuggled a little closer, tucking my cold nose into his throat and chuckling when that caused him to shiver. "Oops, morning Ziame," I said with a grin and he made an adorably grumbling noise while pressing me closer.

Soon we were up, straightening my clothing and surreptitiously checking Ziame's work on the collar in a little more light. I couldn't really tell the difference from before, maybe there were a few scratches on the casing but nothing very noticeable. The three little lights that always blinked red were still glowing so he'd somehow gotten it to work. A look at Sunder who stood at the front of his own cell showed me that it looked identical to his collar.

The two males exchanged a look and when Ziame nodded I realized that the gargoyle male knew about our tampering with the collar. *Okay, that was good right?* If my green guy trusted that scary-looking gargoyle to know our plan that meant he'd have sufficient backup out there today.

I felt like a nervous wreck when the guards came and escorted the males to the gym. When I'd next see Ziame we'd hopefully be free, but what if he didn't make it? What if he got killed in this uprising? I hadn't even thought about that until now, which was stupid. Of course the Krektar would shoot to kill if their lives were at stake and the collar didn't work.

So regardless of who could see I grabbed Ziame's hand and yanked him close, pressing a kiss to the side of his mouth. "For luck!" I whispered and in return, he nuzzled the side of my face and murmured the words back at me. Then he was gone.

When I started nervously pacing while Tori and I waited for our escort to the medical bay even Tori seemed to get agitated. "You're nervous," the young woman said quietly a deep flush rising on her sharp cheekbones.

I paused in my pacing to nod her way. "Yes, I want to get to the Doc, it's cold here," I said, not wanting to make her nervous as well. For effect, I curled my arms more tightly around my middle, like I was trying to hold in my own warmth.

While I was just shy of thirty, poor Tori was barely twenty-two and she was taking this whole kidnapping thing far harder than I was. Of course, I hadn't woken up seven months pregnant, so I didn't know what my mental state would be like if that had happened to me. Unlike Tori I also had a dead-end job, she had a promising start to a career on the stages of Broadway.

It felt like Thonklad was later than normal but maybe it just appeared that way because I was so anxious for this to be done with. There also wasn't any way to tell the time. I wanted to do something, for it to start. It was hard not really being an active part of this escape, I was just on the sidelines and I wouldn't even have a view. I wouldn't know how it went until Ziame reached me in the medical bay.

The Krektar gestured at Tori anxiously, urging her to keep her distance from him but he didn't try to leave her behind again. As we exited the cellblock I followed my routine, working on memorizing the code he typed into the panel to open the door. Even though I likely wouldn't need it at all.

The doctor greeted us cheerily and waved at Thonklad as the guard simply settled outside the door. Then we were inside and Luka was helping Tori sit down on the medical cot which was just a tad high off the ground for her.

Yesterday we'd all realized that Tori didn't have a pain collar on but for the life of us, we hadn't figured out how that could help us escape. Tori was in no shape to traipse through the halls for some sabotage let alone assist in the fighting. Never mind that the poor girl was super timid and shy and barely spoke two words at all around Luka.

As I was too restless to sit I paced around the area and Luka picked up on my tension immediately, "It's happening today?" he asked and I nodded. "We're later this morning than yesterday aren't we?" I asked, worried that the timing was going to be all wrong. Ziame was going to wait three hours before starting the revolt.

Luka shook his head, "No, a little earlier actually, I was worried about you two. I felt like you'd be safer here with me." I didn't say anything in return and simply nodded when Luka asked if that was okay. The timing was going to go wrong, wasn't it? And there was nothing I could do to warn Ziame.

The Doc had focused on his patient, ignoring me. Instead, he scanned Tori's belly again and confirmed what we'd discovered yesterday, the babe was a girl and she wasn't human. Tori had cried when the doctor told her but then she'd tearfully asked if that meant she'd been raped while she'd been out or if she'd simply not remembered. I felt sick at the thought of something like that happening while she'd been unaware and I could see how this had shaken her up.

Luka shrugged helplessly, "I don't know. I think, given the genetic make up of the child that its likely conception was done in a petri dish." Tori nodded as if that made it better and then lapsed into complete, almost catatonic silence for the next, interminable hour.

When the door suddenly opened my heart leaped into my throat, was that Ziame? But no, it was a Krektar who barged into the room, "What's taking so damn long?" he demanded of Luka, Thonklad looking anxiously into the room over the shoulder of the newcomer.

"I was just finishing up with the first female Uru," the doctor said and he gestured at Tori who was still perched on the edge of the medical cot. I understood why he said that, he hoped to buy us another hour but I cringed inwardly. Already predicting just what the Krektar was going to say.

"You finished only one of the girls?" Uru said suspiciously and gazed at where I was frozen from my pacing on the left side of the room. "Of course, I've been working on trying to find a cure for her illness," Luka said smoothly and pointed at Tori, "You don't want to catch what she has and die do you?"

The two Krektar both cringed, but Uru haughtily ordered Thonklad to escort Tori back to her cell now that the Doc was done with her. Then he looked at me again, "And why do you need her?" The Doc had an explanation for that too thankfully. "She's not pregnant yet, I need to tweak the fertility drugs." Uru snorted and gazed at me with a lewd sneer, "Is he sticking it in the right hole at least?"

I flinched at his crudeness and then managed a timid nod which made both Krektar laugh. Uru settled to lean against a nearby wall and Thonklad shook off his dismay at having to escort the possibly contagious Tori back to the cells. I hated this, but I couldn't do a thing to stop it. There was nothing I could say that would sway them, I just had to believe that she'd be safe alone in her cell as much as I was safe in here with the doctor. Even if we now had a guard inside the room.

CHAPTER 8

Ziame

We had to pretend things were normal for a good three hours. All to give my Abigail a chance to reach the doctor's medical bay with the other human. Still, I could tell everyone was on edge, the mood was more subdued, and we were all very focused on our workouts, while surreptitiously glancing at the two guards in the room.

I was in the middle of some bicep curls when Sunder sat down on the bench across from me, he nodded subtly towards the exit. "Geramor is talking with the guards," he said softly, "I don't think that's a good sign. Move now?"

Turning to look I hissed angrily, "Shit, you're right. Yes." I stood and started towards the guards just as the door slid open and several more Krektar started piling into the gym. *Oh, this was bad, this was going to be a blood bath!* The guards all had more weapons, such as blasters and guns besides their shock-sticks, they were prepared for our little uprising.

Geramor grinned an evil smile in my direction and slipped outside in the confusion. With a roar, I ran their way, my fire-starter clicking in my throat as I sprayed a cone of fire over the first two, the unarmed ones.

"Stop! On your knees!" they all yelled at us, even as I saw that my fellow males had followed along and were trying to engage. Then the pain switch was hit and I saw them all thud to the floor, leaving only me standing.

I puffed out all my blades, watched as the Krektar spun on me in confused horror, and swung my tail to decapitate the first. Three down, five to go. They were bringing up their weapons to fire at me, their self-perseverance kicking in over the urge to keep their livestock alive. I ducked, snatched a pain controller off the belt of the nearest fallen, and pressed the off switch.

Then a blast hit me hard in the shoulder and I staggered, dipped my knees, and swung my horns. Bashing the first one in the wall and then impaling the next. It was enough, the other gladiators had risen and were taking care of the rest. The Krektar, even armed were no match for the seven of us.

When the dust settled I looked around, "Everyone alive?" There were six still standing, including myself. Then Kitan bent down on one knee and touched his fingers to the throat of his friend Pu'il and shook his head with a grim look on his face. A gaping hole had been opened up in the red male's chest, a double hit from one of the blasters.

"Damn it," I growled but the Sune male shook his head,

"It's alright. Pu'il died free, he was at peace with this." The orange-furred male rose to his feet and appraised the carnage around us. "Let's get ourselves armed and finish taking over this bloody ship. I'm ready to be free of this thing!" he fingered his pain collar.

"I'll take a pain controller, I'm unaffected so I can keep pressing the button even when they hit the switch." Then I told them to divide the weapons they were comfortable using among themselves. I knew that I wouldn't be any good at fighting with a blaster or gun. In the arena, we all fought with melee weapons, but most were of the opinion that point-and-shoot should work.

"Frek's probably on the bridge, we need to get control of that place or he'll start closing bulkheads or such," I warned the others. Then I ducked my head out the door and looked both ways, it was empty right now but I had no clue which way the bridge was. I knew which way led back to the cells though so I opted to head the other way.

My shoulder ached and burned but the hit was superficial, my scales had absorbed most of the blast even if they were a little charred around the edges. I could tell from the way some of my cohorts were moving behind me that they hadn't all been so lucky when the guns had gone off but we were all committed now.

"We should split up, likely the doctor and the women are safe in the medical bay but we need to make sure. There's probably at least one Krektar there," I said and Sunder gave me a sharp nod and gestured at one of the others to follow him, splitting off and heading down a different hallway as we came to a split.

Kitan seemed to know the way, gesturing us toward the

bridge with a feral grin. "She's a beauty, this ship. I had a feeling it was a Star Class Cruiser from the sound of the engines but these damn pirates made an abysmal mess of her." I didn't care one way or another, as long as he could fly the ship and we could get control of her.

At the doors to the bridge, we pressed our backs to either side of the hallway, Kitan across from me with a hand over the access panel. "Ready?" I asked them, watching the two in the back raise their guns and nod with grim looks on their faces. They knew they'd be hit with the pain controller if they didn't kill everyone in the first round but they were ready for it anyway.

Kitan hissed quietly, "Try not to hit any panels or we're screwed, I doubt any of us are capable of fixing her if we mess something up." A comforting thought, the last thing I wanted was to be stranded out in space if we blew a critical panel to smithereens.

Raising my hand I counted down from three and on zero Kitan hit the panel and we swept onto the bridge. There were three Krektar present, one of them the inexperienced Thonklad and one of them Frek who was scrawny and cowardly.

Guns went off as we surprised them and all three hit the deck, I didn't know if they were all hit or if it was a reflex. the next moment the pain switch was hit and my three fellow gladiators dropped to the floor as well. Possibly they could resist the pain but in this case, it was smarter to go down when vulnerable and present a less obvious target.

I switched the control off and whirled to see Frek scramble to his feet, clearly unharmed, and try to make a run for it. He was headed for the ready room across the bridge and I managed to swipe him good across his back with my tail. He screamed in pain and stumbled but then the door slid shut behind him, my claws grazing the door instead.

There was a scream behind me and I spun, ready to dive into the fray, just in time to see Kitan face the third Krektar. His arm got hit with a shock-stick and he crumpled, several blasts going off at the same time. Both Kitan and the Krektar dropped like stones, smoke curling from their bodies.

No! Shit no! I groaned, not wanting to lose another of the males. They were my brothers in arms now, they'd thrown their lot behind mine, so I was responsible. Whirling around I located the last adversary, filled with anger, ready to rend him to pieces.

Deflating just as quickly when I saw the other two males had cornered Thonklad behind one of the consoles and the Krektar male was actually sobbing, arms curled around his head. I caught a look from one of the gladiators, Fierce I thought his name was, it was a little disgusted and confused. Clearly, just like me, neither male felt comfortable killing a prone and terrified target.

"Secure him," I said instead, and with a look of relief, the two started complying. "Watch the damn ready room and shoot Frek if he makes an appearance." Then I bent down and slung Kitan over my shoulder, the male was badly hurt, dying. Maybe if I got him to the Doc in time he'd be able to save him. A male could hope.

I followed my nose as much as I could but I had to backtrack twice, my scales twitching at the loss of time. Securing the ship was important and it wasn't done, with Frek barricaded in the ready room I knew he could still do us some damage. Saving Kitan's life if at all possible was just as important though.

My jaw firmed in determination and tendrils of fire blew from my nostrils. *I could do this! I would save us all. I wasn't going to lose another male.*

ᔕ

Abigail

Luka made a good show of having me lie down on the cot and slowly scanning each portion of my body. Lying through his teeth he claimed I had internal bleeding and bruising and set about 'fixing' me up. The comments had made Uru laugh so I guess it was believable.

The next thirty minutes were filled with fake healing procedures, mostly with the handheld scanner thankfully, and research and re-synthesizing things at the panel next to the bed. Luka took a blood sample twice to supposedly confirm a theory. I was starting to worry he had to actually give me a shot again like that first night when the door suddenly slid open.

My heart soared in elation, yes! That was the cavalry, they had secured the bridge! Then I realized it was Geramor and he was by himself. The blue-furred male glared at us all, his eyes firmly settling on Uru who'd straightened and was reaching for the pain controller.

Geramor's mouth stretched open freakishly wide, showing off rows upon rows of terrifying shark-like teeth. Uru squealed in fear but the switch was hit and I saw the attacking gladiator twitch in pain. Saw Uru's look of victory.

I rose, searching for the nearest weapon but Luka beat me

to the punch. The doctor was on Uru with such quick stealth I barely saw him move at all. Then he jabbed a hypodermic needle into the Krektar's neck and with a hiss, the male collapsed. Immediately, he grabbed the controller and turned off Geramor's collar.

Luka didn't know of Ziame's distrust of this male and didn't know that I didn't trust this either. Why was Geramor here and not Ziame? I couldn't imagine he'd send anyone in his stead, except maybe Sunder. Far more likely, they'd think we were safe in here and wouldn't come until the bridge was secure.

My suspicions were confirmed when Geramor rounded on Luka, his mouth closing down to normal proportions. "Take off my collar Doc, now!" he ordered and his foot snapped out so quick it blurred, spinning the pain controller Luka had been holding right out of his hand.

He was tugging the weapons off Uru's belt the next moment and rounding on us, blaster raised. "Hurry the fuck up!" he snarled with menace. Luka stared at him for a moment, his black eyes wide open and then he slid a look at me as if asking *me* for permission. At my silent nod and rather helpless shrug he moved to a cabinet and pulled out some tools.

Germamor was pacing back and forth, casting an anxious look at the door behind him, and then rudely urging the doctor to hurry up. My eyes darted to the pain controller he'd kicked away, it had landed in a corner and I started to very slowly drift that way, trying to make it look like I wasn't really moving.

When Luka told Germamor to sit down in front of him so he could get at the collar the shaggy blue male lifted the blaster and pressed it right up against the doctor's chest, "No funny business! Or I shoot your heart out."

To my shock, the Doc's mouth lifted into a smirk and then he shifted his body, "Then you need to aim a little more to the right, yeah like that. My heart's on the right side." I nearly stifled a hysterical laugh at the angry, slightly baffled look the shaggy blue-haired gladiator gave Luka.

Then my foot was on the controller and I hesitated, wait any longer and Luka would have the collar off and the controller would be useless. If I pressed that damn button now would it cause him to blast a hole in Luka's chest? I couldn't risk it, we couldn't afford to be hurtling through space without a healer.

I think that the doctor was trying to move as slowly as possible when he opened up the collar, stalling for time. But eventually, the thing dropped from Geramor's throat and the male was free. He immediately raised the blaster and cold-cocked Luka in the face so that the doctor collapsed on the floor with a strangled yelp. He didn't get up.

"You are coming with me," Geramor barked my way and he approached and grabbed me firmly by the arm, starting to haul me out the door. I dug in my feet, slipping and sliding across the floor on my heels, sadly, though beautiful they did not provide adequate traction. With another firm yank, I stumbled out of the medical room with Geramor.

Changing tracks I followed him, my heels clicking on the metal flooring, "Where are you taking me? We're on a spaceship, there's nowhere to run." Unless there was actually something like a smaller ship docked or in a hangar bay or something? An escape pod? Didn't ships have those in sci-fis?

The shaggy blue male didn't deign to give me an answer,

simply hurrying me along through several hallways, some lined with doors, some not. I was lost within seconds but sadly he seemed to know just where he was headed.

I tried again, "Seriously where are we going? Why are you taking me?" But the guy stonewalled me completely until we, at last, reached some kind of hangar bay where it looked like two smaller ships were indeed parked.

With a sinking feeling, I realized I was seriously about to be kidnapped a second time this week. If this asshole got me off this ship I knew I was done for, I doubted that Ziame would be able to find me then. I had to stop this somehow.

"Why would you even take me? Ziame, also known as the Beast, he's going to murder your ass. You get that right?" I said, hoping to get some kind of response from him. He was still holding onto me tightly with one hand and working on a panel beside a door in the side of the shuttle. When it slid open I dug in my heels again, fighting to keep him from dragging me aboard.

It was no use though, Geramor was simply too strong and he didn't care about harming me either. With an angry snarl, he picked me up and hurled me into the ship. I rolled over the floor, slid a good three feet, and then slammed hard into some metal paneling.

I saw stars, my head throbbing from the impact, and my body aching all over. The sound of my pain finally loosened his tongue though; he laughed while he headed for the pilot's seat at the front. One look at the door showed me it was closed.

"We are leaving, I am not sticking around with those uptight morally righteous freaks. If I do I'll never get a decent meal." He swung his head around, maw gaping disturbingly my way. As if it wasn't clear he meant that I was a decent meal, he actually stuck out a black tongue and licked his lips.

Then he faced the front again and started his pre-flight check or whatever it was. Flicking buttons and lighting up panels, the engines vibrated to life. *Damn it! Shit! Fuck!* This was not going right. It was just my damn luck to instigate an uprising and then get taken by a flesh-eating monster.

"Of course, if you're actually pregnant from that obnoxious idiot you'll make me a fortune. Guess you're in luck and I won't eat you just yet," he muttered in an aside. His attention was on the controls, I didn't think he thought I was much of a threat. He was right of course, even though I was tall for a human woman, I was on the small side next to this asshole. Ziame had only a little in height on Geramor, though he had far more bulk.

"Geez, what a relief," I said, trying to keep him distracted while I searched for a weapon. "Get eaten now or sold into slavery later along with my child. Fun choices!" I pitched my voice bright and bubbly as if I was talking about flavors of ice cream and saw how Geramor looked over his shoulder at me in confusion. I guess sarcasm was lost on this guy.

Everything in the shuttle appeared either bolted to the floor or tucked behind a panel. There was no handy fireman box with an ax tucked behind a glass pane. The ship started rumbling louder and I could feel the floor vibrate beneath me. *I was running out of time, I had to act now!*

Slipping off my heels so I wouldn't make noise when walking, I fingered the sharply pointed stiletto. *Was I really doing this?* I eyed the hulking monster in the chair at the front, what was his weak spot? Where did I even hit this guy?

It needed to be final, I couldn't fight him, and injuring him would probably just enrage him enough to actually eat me.

I tiptoed to my feet, heading his way, keeping my heels low at my sides so he wouldn't think anything of them if he saw me. I held my breath, terrified he'd lift off before I got to him, terrified he'd see me and I'd fail, and terrified I'd hit him and it wouldn't be enough.

I reached his chair quietly, black spots dancing in front of my eyes. *Breathe Abigail, breathe!* You can do this. Then I raised my shoe, eyed his face, and then aimed the pointed heel straight for his bat-like ears.

It sank in far too easily for my liking as if there was no resistance at all; maybe that was my adrenaline. The blue-haired freak let out a hair-raising squeal and stumbled out of the pilot's chair, turning on me with one clawed hand raised.

I ducked, stumbling backward to avoid that deadly swipe. *Oh no, it wasn't a killing blow.* I was *so* screwed! I felt a searing pain across my chest as his claws raked me, losing my balance I fell backward and Geramor with an angry growl lunged at me. His weight landed heavily on top of me, the air rushing out of my lungs, my head spinning from its second blow to the floor.

Panicked I raised my fist and hit him, grazing the stiletto still dug into his ear, his entire body jerked on top of me. That hurt, he was so heavy I couldn't breathe but he wasn't clawing at me and he'd stopped growling. In fact, he might have stopped breathing too.

CHAPTER 9

Ziame

Kitan wasn't breathing, at least, I didn't think he was. I dug my clawed feet into the metal flooring, leaving grooves as I raced for the medbay. I had to believe Abigail when she said the doctor on this ship was on our side, had to believe he'd save the Sune male.

Bursting into the medbay, I was met with two stunned males, one of them Jakar who had accompanied Sunder here. The other was unfamiliar to me but it was an Aderian male so he had to be the doctor, and just like Abigail had told me, he wore a slave collar.

Derailed as I was, I still hurried to place Kitan on the medical cot and I didn't even need to ask or say anything.

The Adarian male was already there, scanning him, pressing instructions to the medical bed and the surgery arm in its panel at the head of the table. "Not good," he murmured, "But I've got a pulse, I can work with that."

I wasn't even on the male's radar as he assumed responsibility for his patient. I turned on Jakar, "Where's Abigail?" The male leaned toward me, clasped my shoulder in a firm grip with one of his four arms, eyes concerned. That wasn't good, it made my hearts beat fervently in my chest, worry for my female flooding me.

"Geramor abducted her after he killed Uru and made the Doc take off his collar." One of his many hands pointed at the corpse in the corner and then at the discarded pain collar on the floor. There was a flush of color riding the spots that marked his cheeks, but I wasn't sure what that meant.

"No!" I roared, panic creating a kind of static in my brain, I couldn't lose my female. I had to get her back! If Geramor had her, he might very well eat her, a fate worse than death. I struggled to get my breathing under control while I spun toward the door, fire was curling away from my face, my fire-starter clicking angrily in my throat with each exhale. I was starting to get dizzy, burning up my oxygen instead of breathing it.

"Sunder is after her, we weren't far behind, he'll get your female back," Jakar was saying but the sound of his voice came from far away. All I heard was a rushing in my ears, I flicked them back angrily. Then I darted my tongue out of my mouth to catch Abigail's scent, the forked tip curling as it tasted her pheromones in the air.

Then I rushed out the door, her scent strong in my nose, just like that of Geramor and Sunder, it was easy to trace their steps. I reached what had to be the hangar bay after a few twists and turns. I wasn't surprised, of course, Geramor would try to make a run for it and this was the only way how. It did surprise me that he'd known where to go and that he thought he knew how to use the short-range shuttlecraft.

The door was open and I was able to spot two small short-range spacecraft inside the bay, the big airlock wasn't opened which I took as a good sign. Which craft were they in? Or had Geramor already taken off? Was I too late? My heart sank and my fire-starter clicked again, fire curling from my nostrils.

"Ziame!" That was Abigail calling my name, I spun towards the sound and spotted her perched on some crates near the back wall. Sunder was hovering at her side, one wing outstretched and curved around her but not touching. The protective posture rattled my spines nonetheless but the moment he saw me the wing dropped away.

I hurried to her and only at the last moment realized that the hangar bay was brightly lit and Abigail could see me in my full glory. My ears flicked down, drooping, and all my spines flattened, the blades on my arms tucking themselves in. The last thing I wanted to do was frighten her but I couldn't help how I looked, and it was a fact of life that a full-grown Lacerten male terrified even males like Sunder. Point in case, the stone-skin male had taken several steps back at my approach.

But Abigail, my brave Abigail, she actually jumped off her perch and stumbled toward me. Leaping into my arms and tucking herself close, "Ziame! You're alive, thank God!" Her warm weight against mine, her soft curves pressing against my body, immediately my world righted itself. We'd made it.

We'd done it!

I pressed her close, nuzzled my nose into her springy curls, and tasted her sweet, sweet pheromones with my tongue. "Are you alright?" I asked her, my eyes scanning over her shoulder to check her back. There was no blood there, but I tasted the coppery tang of it in the air.

She nodded, "A little banged up, a few scratches. I'm okay." Each scratch and bruise was one mark too many but she was breathing, alive, and in my arms. I could deal with the rest. "Are you?" she asked, pulling back to look me over and gasping at the blast mark on my shoulder and the gash on my thigh I'd sustained in the fighting.

"I'm fine little one," I said, "Barely hurts at all." Then my sharp gaze took in the slashes across her chest, from collarbone to the top of her breasts. Through her blouse and jacket, marring her luscious dark skin, three lines were welling gently with blood. "You are hurt!"

Frantic I pulled the fabric away, trying to see how bad the marks were, and was met with laughter. "It's alright, he barely scratched me, it looks far worse than it is."I was about to say it looked bad enough, my heart was pounding with worry, but she probably wouldn't like hearing that, I didn't want to frighten her.

It was Sunder who actually calmed me, "She is alright, if you had scratches like that you wouldn't even notice them." Forcing myself to look at the scratches more objectively I had to nod, "Okay, alright. You're alright." That still didn't mean I liked it, nothing should ever mar her beautiful skin if I could help it.

I was rewarded with a bright smile from my Abigail and then she tucked herself back against my body. When she did that this time I noticed the difference in height, my beautiful female had shrunk. Squinting over the top of her head and shoulders down at her feet I noticed that her stilts were gone; instead, she was barefoot.

"Where are your shoes?" I asked and because of my proximity, a shiver ran over her delicate spine beneath my hands. I swung her up into my arms, raising her easily so that we could look each other in the eye.

Now she didn't look happy, she looked sad. "I killed Geramor with them." I stared in confusion, she killed Geramor with her shoes? *She what?* I couldn't for the life of me picture it. Over her shoulder, Sunder mimed stabbing himself in the ear and I had a vivid picture flash through my brain of the narrow sharp spike on the heel of her odd footwear. *Ouch.*

Somehow I'd assumed that Sunder had rescued her but it seemed like she'd rescued herself, my whole body flushed with pride. Then understanding followed, the first kill was the hardest, it had shaken me up badly the first time I'd been forced to kill. And she really, really liked those crazy shoes, she'd barely taken them off at all since I met her and lovingly polished them with the corner of the blanket each morning.

"We'll get you some new shoes at the first chance," I said confidently, and if no vendors sold footwear like that I'd commission someone to make some. I beamed at her when she gave a wet chuckle and then added more seriously, "I'm proud of you. You saved yourself. I know this is hard but when it's kill or be killed you have no choice. I for one am glad about this outcome."

She raised a soft hand to place against my cheek and then she stroked her fingers up and tugged gently on one of my long ears. "Thank you Ziame, that's sweet of you. I'm pretty glad too and I suppose if I hadn't killed the bastard he'd have gone on to eat some other poor hapless person..."

The growl was out before I could stop it, "He was going to eat you?" I should have known, she must have been so scared. I almost wished he wasn't dead yet so I could take care of it myself, *slowly*. My tough female was beaming a smile at me again, her shoulders rolling in a shrug.

"If I wasn't pregnant." Then she wiggled her eyebrows at me, "Which I'm not, I think we need to get some practice in on that." My body flushed with heat and I was suddenly far too aware of all the points of contact her body made on mine. Her side pressed against my belly, the curve of her bottom on my hip. Her legs draped over my arm, the soft curve of her breast pressed against my ribs. Her luminous eyes as they stared straight into mine, without flinching.

Sunder coughed, "Hate to interrupt but eh… Did everyone make it? Is the ship secure?" His words doused the flames, Kitan's life was still in the balance and Frek had barricaded himself in the ready room. The ship was in fact *not* secure at all. I explained both these things to them and informed Abigail of the sad loss of Pu'il's life in the first skirmish down in the gym. Then we discussed various options on how to get Frek out of that room and either dead or off the ship.

It never came to that, Frek took matters into his own hands when his voice came through over the ship's intercom, cackling gleefully. "I know you think you've won, you bastards," he said. "But you haven't. I've got the cellblock isolated with one pretty, pregnant human inside it. Stand down now and surrender and I won't deprive her of her precious oxygen."

There was a moment of stunned silence among the three of us, a moment which Frek gave us to let the news sink in. "I think a human can last four minutes without oxygen before permanent damage sets in. Your time starts now. I'm waiting!" He spoke with such malicious cheer, that it almost sounded like he *wanted* to kill the pregnant female.

No! We couldn't let Tori die but to have all our lives locked back into slavery? To have Pu'il die for nothing? That was intolerable too. I just had to glance at the collar around Abigail's throat to know how much I abhorred the thought of her in slavery.

Abigail squirmed in my arms, "Put me down! We need to hurry to the cellblock. I know the access code!" I spun, disobeying her order, and started running. Aware that Sunder had already rushed out of the hangar bay ahead of us the moment Frek spoke his hateful words. "We're faster like this," I said and leaned into the sprint, claws digging at the floor with each leap.

I followed Sunder's scent, knowing he was headed the same way, and soon recognized the hallway leading to our previous prison. Sunder was at the door panel. Claws dug into the frame, trying hard to somehow yank the bulkhead open. It was no use, I'd tried that very thing on the other side of the door when I'd made a break for it when they first brought us here. My horns had made two nice little dents in the panel on the other side, but the door hadn't budged.

Skidding to a stop I let Abigail down and she dove for the access panel, her slender fingers typing in the ten-digit code as if she was a native of the Krektar numeric system. Sunder and I both held our breath in anticipation, the moment the door slid open, the air got sucked into the oxygen-deprived room in a rush. When the crack was big enough the stone-skinned male hurried through.

Tori had been locked in the first cell on the right and she had slumped against the front bars. Since Frek had vented her oxygen from the room about a minute had passed and she was sluggish and weak. Fearing that Frek would attempt to lock us in again I stayed in the opened door panel and watched as Sunder strained to break the bars on her cell.

A few cells down the bond broken Ferai beast let out a plaintive howl, as if it felt sympathetic to the poor female's plight. Then it started pacing, having managed the no-air situation far better than the small pregnant human.

As soon as Sunder bent two bars apart far enough to reach for the female he pulled her to safety and then we all retreated. "Shit, that was close!" Abigail said while she crouched on the dirty floor beside the female and checked her pulse and breathing. "Tori, are you okay? Can you hear me?"

The small female nodded weakly and I could see her pulse flutter in her throat. Sunder rumbled at her, "I'm going to pick you up female, and bring you to the doctor. Just to make sure." Tori didn't say a thing, just pressed her mouth in a thin line and allowed Sunder to carry her. Her skin was deathly pale, almost white, and with her long blonde hair, she looked almost like a wraith, especially in contrast to Sunder's nearly black stone-like skin.

I eyed Abigail who was standing on the dirt-encrusted floor in her bare feet, "I assume you'll want to stay by Tori's side?" She needed to calm the female help her. I knew I needed to get to the bridge and help the others decide on our next course of action, especially now that Kitan could not fly this ship.

Mind made up, I lifted her into my arms and hurried after Sunder and his burden; I needed to check in with the Doc anyway before I could make any informed choices. More than anything I also wanted to see the pain collars removed from Abigail and me.

The doctor looked up when we entered with relief evident on his face. He was still working on Kitan. With Jakar standing across from him and kitted out in gloves as well, dark red blood staining the fingers of his gloves; promoted to nurse it seemed. "Put her over there, how long was she without?" the doctor said, checking off a final thing on the panel of the medical bot. Then he was hurrying over, stripping his gloves as he came to assist Sunder in putting the female down on the second cot, one without the medical arm.

A flashlight was procured which he shone in her eyes and he started scanning her with his handheld. "All is well," he said but he pulled out an oxygen mask all the same to administer some extra. "Keep that on for five minutes Tori."

Then he stepped back, letting Abigail and Sunder fuss over the pregnant female, and addressed me. "I understand Kitan was supposed to fly this ship?" At my nod, he sighed, "I'm afraid he's not going anywhere for the next three days at least. Guess that means we're dead in the water?"

I pointed at my collar, "How quick can you get this off?" Those fathomless black eyes didn't blink, he just reached for some tools and his scanner and immediately got to work. Long-fingered hands deftly working on the clasp around my neck.

"Soon," he said, "What's next? How are we getting out of here?" It was clear the Adarian male was worried. His eyes darted from fumbling with my collar to where Kitan was stretched out, unconscious on the medical cot while the surgical arm was working on him.

"I can fly small craft, I can probably figure this out," I said with more confidence than I felt. The collar dropped away from my throat with immense satisfaction and I grinned, "Thanks Doc. Get back to your patients, I'll take Sunder and talk with the other two still on the bridge. We'll get this sorted."

ര

Abigail

Ziame had left for the bridge the moment his collar had dropped from his throat. I only knew he was gone because his tail had uncurled from my leg, but he hadn't said a word. I wasn't sure if I was feeling hurt over that or not, he had important things to take care of and I knew Tori needed me to stay with her.

Except she fell asleep shortly after, clearly exhausted from all that had transpired and Jakar and Luka had finished with Kitan so the Doc was now working on getting Jakar's collar off. Once it dropped away I swear it looked like the big gladiator actually struggled not to cry. He took in a deep breath, looked at Luka, and me and then left.

After that Luka had me watch closely while he took off the collar still around Kitan's throat and then insisted I return the favor for his own collar. My hands shook as I did the work; a surgeon or mechanic I was not. Luka was all business afterward, working on releasing the collar from my neck with quick practiced moves. Nothing like how he'd struggled when working on Geramor.

"Go on, get to the bridge now, I'll take care of our patients," Luka told me when I was free. I had to admit that even I felt a little emotional after the hated thing dropped from my skin. I'd only been a slave for three days, Ziame for example had been one for three years, it must have been quite something to finally be free. I fully understood why Jakar had looked like he'd been filled with emotion when he was released.

Finding my way to the bridge took far longer than I expected, mostly because I got lost three times and had to backtrack. The ship was far bigger than I expected, there were three decks and endless hallways to traverse. I thought that most of them held crew quarters, one even sounded like someone was banging on a door. I'd also walked past something that looked kind of like a science lab and I wondered just what kind of ship this used to be.

When I finally located the bridge I found all the gladiators who were up and running standing around it, discussing options. Ziame was leaning over one of the many consoles that lined the half-round room. "Near as I can tell I should be able to engage the autopilot that will fly us to the already set destination. Xio."

The others fell silent and shared long looks, I didn't know what Xio was but I gathered nothing good. As I stepped further inside Ziame settled his green gaze on mine, dipping his head and flicking his ears in greeting. Unsure of my place in this meeting I started his way and was happy when he stood and easily tucked me under his brawny arm; his tail finding its usual spot, curled around one of my ankles.

"Abigail, glad you joined us," he said, his deep voice rumbling against my side. I wasn't normally the type that wanted to have her boyfriend constantly touching her, having her man propping her up, but it was nice to have Ziame include me like this. I didn't know where I stood with any of these other males, some still looked pretty feral and terrifying to me.

"Hi," I said and then I added, "I think maybe we should do a round of introductions first. I don't know any of you... But if we're going to be sharing a ship, for now, I'd like to." Maybe it was silly to say that, but honestly? What was I going to do? I needed to get to know these guys.

There was some chuckling and then Sunder, who was the only one whose name I knew by now, spoke up. "Good idea Abby, a round of names, real or gladiator, whatever you want us to address you as. Plus if you have an applicable skill, maybe mention that too."

Ziame went first, saying how he could fly small ships and knew the basics of mechanics, which was useful, and a specialty in anthropology, which wasn't as much. He admitted openly to the others that his species was highly advanced and had hidden from the rest of the galaxy and he'd like it to stay that way. There were some solemn vows that they would and then Sunder moved on, he'd been a gladiator the longest, having been a trainer of new ones for nearly fifteen years and it seemed he easily slipped into a kind of counseling role.

As the greetings went on, with Jakar, Fierce, and Thorin, it became evident that none of the others knew even remotely how to fly a ship. Ziame was the closest thing, let alone the difficult job of navigating, it was a very select skill. Then Thorin raised another issue, *money.*

Ziame was scrubbing at the spiked ridge on his head, clearly frustrated. I understood how he felt, we weren't safe when we had no money, no supplies, and no ability to fly this ship. As long as we were floating in space it was unlikely we'd be found but at some point, we had to get more food. It was probably best to at least vacate our last known position in case Frek had managed to get off a message to his boss.

"Okay, here's a really crazy idea," I said. "What's our most marketable skill as a group? These gladiator fights. Am I right?" At the nods and interested looks, I squared my shoulders and continued on, "So what if we still head for Xio? That's our current heading and Ziame can get us going that way at least right?"

There were uncomfortable looks now, especially from Sunder but Ziame had caught on. "We pretend we're still owned by Drameil, win our fights and collect the purses in his name. By that time Kitan might be healed enough to get us going and maybe we can pick up an actual navigator while we're there."

Sunder nodded, "That sounds like a solid plan, most of the fights planned weren't death matches right? Only mine?" I swallowed in shock, "Oh no Sunder, you can't fight then! We're not letting you kill another enslaved gladiator." The barbaric practice was really sinking in now and I felt sick to my stomach for even suggesting this hare-brained idea.

Fierce smiled a wide-toothed, fanged smile at me and chuckled while Sunder scratched at the crown of short horns circling his head, was he embarrassed? "Thank you Abby for the vote of confidence, but eh... I was the one set to die in that fight." My horrified gasp filled the silence on the bridge.

I stared at the gargoyle-like male while I tried to understand what he was saying. "What do you mean you were set to die?" There was a really bad taste forming in my mouth now. Was he saying these fights were rigged? Or just his?

With his arm around my shoulder, Ziame squeezed me to him gently, "It's very common for a portion of the fights to be rigged. That way owners make a lot more money on them. Sometimes when we head into the arena we're told to lose, sometimes we're purposely set up in unfair fights and sometimes it's a way to get rid of an obsolete or obstinate slave."

Eyes wide I looked at the muscular, stone-skinned Sunder with his large wings. "And you've been obstinate is that it?" Now the male laughed, his slate-gray eyes twinkling, "I am old female, far older than the rest of the males here, I was a trainer for the past fifteen years, not a gladiator. I pissed off Drameil and so here I am, slated to die."

With the stone skin, I couldn't possibly tell how old Sunder was and he looked to me as fit and muscular as any of the others. I eyed him a little more closely, but no, I really couldn't tell. It seemed the male took pity on me, "This is my stone-skin form, battle-form if you will. You'd see gray hairs when I shift back if I could but I've gotten stuck." He shrugged and made a 'what-you-see-is-what-you -get' gesture.

Oh, okay, Sunder had another shape that he couldn't reach right now. That was hard to wrap my mind around. "Sunder's not the only fight that's out, obviously Kitan is too and so is Pu'il," Ziame said solemnly, and at the mention of

Pu'il's name, I saw all of the gladiators raise their fist and tap it to their chest in a gesture of respect.

"And I don't know about you guys," Thorin said after a respectful pause, "But I don't feel comfortable putting the Ferai beast in a fight either. It has no ability to choose this at all." The others all made sounds of confirmation and my respect for the former slaves rose. Some of them might look beastly and they'd terrified me that first night, now they were showing they were good men at heart.

"Okay, so how many fighters does that give us?" Ziame asked. "Five?" he guessed and then shook his head, "No, our Abby here killed Geramor so that leaves four out of nine. That's not good." I cringed at the reminder, vividly recalling the way my heel had sunk into the bastard's ear canal. I really thought for long seconds that he'd actually lived through that but he'd collapsed on top of me in his death throes. If not for Sunder's timely arrival I would have suffocated under the heavy weight.

"So we say we've been attacked by pirates and lost half our fighters. I mean part of that is true, right?" I suggested. How common were pirate attacks, was that a believable excuse? I didn't really like that they were actually contemplating my stupid idea, so I was kind of glad that it had Ziame shake his head.

"They'll believe that but they'll still try to keep us to the right amount of fighters. They'll lose money if they don't. These fights get promoted months in advance sometimes. Some of us have a reputation, a fan base, they make trading cards about us for kids."

I groaned, shit this universe was a sick place. Trading cards for kids on gladiators? I suppose this was like baseball to aliens. “Then what? Xio is not an option then is it?” I sighed, “Okay we’ll need to figure out the navigation and a safer destination.” I eyed the console with the holographic star charts hovering over it. That was all about calculations, wasn’t it? Maybe I could figure it out somehow… If only I could read the damn alien script.

“Or,” Ziame said, “I’ll offer to fight all of them on my own. Six to one, or two fights back to back, three to one.” *No! Hell no!* Was my instant response and from the stunned looks on the faces of the others, I thought maybe they were thinking the same. I was about to object when Sunder nodded thoughtfully.

“That could work, what do we know of the opponents they’d paired the dropouts with? The organizers will probably prefer the two back-to-back fights, more air time. Can you sustain combat that long?” he said while he raised a hand and started ticking off fingers. “I was slated to fight Doom, big, long reach and thick skin. He’s a Kertinal.”

Fierce added, “Kitan and Pu’il were set for a team fight against a set of Asrai twins. Telepathic those two but no flight and no armor. You can probably fry them with your breath.” The others also listed the remaining three combatants and were clearly considering this doable so I had to interfere.

“Hell no! Are you even listening? No one’s risking Ziame in a fight six to one! No amount of money is worth that!” I yelled. Then in the stunned silence that followed, I swung on the hulking male at my side and poked his scaly chest. “Stop it, I know this was my idea in the first place but I don’t want any of you taking risks! We’re doing this to live our lives free! To be happy! Not to run off and get ourselves killed for money just so some jackasses are entertained!”

Ziame eyed the other males over my shoulder and then took me by the hand, "Excuse us for a moment," he said and towed me with him into a room off the bridge. There was a large smear of blood on one wall that I eyed apprehensively. In explanation, he said, "Fierce and Thorin got into the ready room and took care of Frek at around the same time we rescued Tori." Then he firmly turned me so my back was to it.

"I understand your fear little Abigail," he said, bending down a good foot so he could better look me in the eye. "But we're not talking death matches here. These are fights until the win is obvious or until one opponent admits defeat. This is my last chance to fight in the arena for us as well. I am the only one of my kind, show up at a fight, and Drameil will know it's me and come looking. After this fight, I'll never step foot in the arena again. Let me do this for my brothers, alright?"

Worry was still my most prevalent emotion but I could hear what he was saying and what he was promising me. I kept seeing images of him lying dead on the sands of some arena (in my head it was the Colosseum as that was the only arena I knew). It was irrational and far too quick to feel what I was feeling for him but I was.

This wasn't love, not yet, but it could be eventually, and damn it I wanted that. I wanted to have Ziame for myself and to make this work somehow, in space. I knew I couldn't go back home, I'd seen too much, changed. I didn't know how long I'd been gone but I could guess it was far longer than just a few weeks.

"Ziame," I sighed and shook my head, "You can't get hurt. What would I do then?" Oh man that sounded so clingy and needy I actually cringed but when a smile broke out on his face I couldn't regret saying it.

He curved his hands around my face and leaned in, pressing his forehead to mine. "Abigail, my sweet-smelling, beautiful Abigail," he whispered, "I'll come back to you. Promise. I'm called the Beast for a reason. I've dominated the arena for three years, unbeatable. I'll be alright."

But he didn't promise that he wouldn't get hurt. I guess this was as good as I was going to get.

CHAPTER 10

Ziame

After we'd settled on our course of action, I re-engaged the autopilot on its set course for Xio. This ship was faster than the Caratoa we'd initially traveled on, which was probably the reason the Krektar had risked making a detour. From the nav console, I'd gathered that they'd been to the Yengar space station where they'd bought Abigail and Tori's faulty pods. Despite our two hours hiatus and that detour, we'd still make it just in time.

While I'd worked with the controls, the other gladiators had collected the bodies and thrown them out the airlock. They'd left the two injured Krektar locked in their quarters, stripped of any weapons, and locked Thonklad in the cellblock that had previously housed us. As soon as the two injured ones had gotten a clean bill of health from the Doc, they'd follow the same fate.

Then all the males had apparently found the time to have a private chat because they escorted me to the med bay and then officially voted me Captain. The idiots seemed to think I'd make a good leader for some reason but as Abigail proudly smiled at me I felt my spines flick up in pride a little too. *Okay, I'd give this gig a shot,* I was likely the most educated male in the lot so I guess it did make sense.

Even Kitan, weak and heavily sedated had roused enough to vote for me, they seemed to think that made it unanimous. I was a little surprised when Sunder came over to clasp my shoulder and press his forehead to mine, "You'll do well and I'll try to advise you any way I can." Knowing the male had two decades of experience more than I had, I was glad for the help.

Afterward, I wanted to spend time with Abigail, just for a moment revel in being alone with her with no immediate threats hanging over our heads. But she had other plans for the moment. First having made sure that the doctor had checked each of us for injuries and treated us where necessary; she'd then had one of us pull up the ship's schematic so we could assign quarters and start clean-up.

With fierce determination, she had declared that if we were to be living on this ship for now, it was damn well not going to be a pigsty. Whatever that was… We'd all set off to get on with our various tasks and Abigail had taken Tori to the mess hall to take care of the food.

So while I was cleaning out a cabin I found myself cornered one after the other by each of the males. First, it was Fierce, then Jakar, and last came Thorin, I realized they each just wanted to talk, wanted to get to know me better. I understood, all this time I'd kept my mouth shut and pretended I was a dumb beast while they'd spoken, gotten to know each other.

Sunder was the only one who let me be, at least I thought so but he cornered me just before mealtime, right as I was about to see Abigail again. "I've taken it upon myself to clear out the Captain's quarters," he said, "I know Abigail didn't schedule it but I felt it made sense these quarters went to you. It has a far bigger bed so you should be comfortable." He eyed my horns as he said that and grinned, "Maybe you slide the bed away from the headboard a tad yes?" I would likely have to if I wanted to have space for my horns.

I didn't want to be singled out for preferential treatment but I understood that being the leader, chosen leader at that, came with certain symbols of office so to speak. Besides, part of me was glad to have the use of a bigger bed, I'd eyed the ones I'd seen in the cabins with some trepidation. Sharing one of those with Abigail would be a tight fit. Not that she'd chosen to share my bed yet, for now, she'd assigned herself her own cabin.

"Thank you," I forced myself to say, "I will try to do right by us. In fact, can you go round and check with each male if there's any that wish it and can go home? Once we've got a navigator we could possibly return some of them to where they belong." Sunder nodded, "I'll do that."

Abigail and Tori as it turned out had worked hard to clean up the kitchen and the mess hall so that we could all sit down for a real meal for the first time on this ship. Even the doctor, who told us all to call him Luka, joined us for the meal. It was something the ladies called stew which was the best they could do with what little ingredients they had. They had sounded apologetic about it, but it was the best damn meal we'd had in a long time so the space was filled with nothing but appreciation.

After the meal, things turned to an impromptu celebration; one of the males had found a stash of Adarian wine in one of the cabins and we shared that. It was one of those glowing evenings I'd likely remember fondly for a long time. Tori had sung a few songs for us, Abigail sat next to me all evening and for the first time in three years I was free, and I felt like I belonged. Tomorrow's worries were just that, they were for tomorrow.

Then, when I could tell Abigail was flagging I walked her to the cabin assigned to her, one I'd personally cleaned. She kissed me goodnight with those soft lips of hers and then giggled and tripped over her own feet as she headed for her bed. That was just fucking adorable, she was already affected by the mild drink.

As she'd curled up on the bed, apparently already half asleep I went inside and got a wet cloth from the washroom. Then I cleaned her slightly grubby feet as she'd been walking around barefoot since the shoe incident. Noting the pretty pink paint on her dainty little toes, not a single natural weapon on her body, and yet, she'd taken out a fully grown Hoxiam. *I was so damn proud.*

She was snoring softly by the time I had her, still fully dressed, tucked into the bed. Only then did I head off to find her an alternative for footwear.

ᔕ

Abigail

Whatever was in that Adarian wine hit harder than a ton of bricks. Crikey, that stuff was still hammering around in my skull. I sat up with a wince and then had to hold my head as I waited for the world to stop spinning around me. At least my stomach was behaving. When I got up I padded barefoot to the washroom and took the longest, warmest most well-deserved shower ever.

I'd brushed my clothes clean best I could and washed my panties in the sink, going bare for the moment. My feet however… That was a problem. My precious heels were still in the hangar bay and honestly, they could stay there. But yesterday it hadn't been pleasant to walk around barefoot in this still mostly disgusting ship all afternoon. I didn't really feel like doing that again.

With no other option, I headed for my door, fully intending to head for the mess hall so I could help out Tori with breakfast like we'd agreed yesterday. It was a rather domestic division of labor but we girls had decided that it was very likely we were in fact the only ones who knew how to prepare food.

There was a present waiting for me in the hallway though, right in front of my door. Two pairs of far too large socks and a pair of boots, also too big but possibly the smallest pair available onboard this ship. I knew immediately that Ziame had arranged for this and my heart just about melted in my chest, that was so sweet. Who knew I'd be so damn happy with a couple of socks and a pair of ugly boots? When I put on both pairs of socks the boots even almost fit.

I entered the mess hall and a smell that almost resembled bacon greeted my nostrils making my belly rumble in appreciation. I found Tori behind the alien stove, frying strips of something that looked horrifyingly green and turned out to be a kind of vegetable. It was what made the bacon smell and when I tasted it, it was almost right. *Close enough.* I moaned in pleasure, "Where the hell did you find this? Are you a goddess or what?"

Tori graced me with a shy smile, her cheeks going red, "Luka brought it to me. He says he spent the night cataloging all the fresh food in storage and making sure it was safe for all of us to eat..." Then she ducked her head, blonde hair swinging forward to hide her face. "I think he feels guilty for hurting us."

I jumped up and sat down on the nearest counter while I surveyed the breakfast prep Tori had already taken care of. There were several trays of what looked like biscuits, only these were made of some kind of red flour. I spotted blue scrambled eggs to go along with the plate of green bacon she was preparing now. "Tori, how long have you been up to do all this? I thought we'd work on it together." The girl was pregnant, she shouldn't be working too hard.

She shrugged, "Apparently this baby likes to kick me awake in the early hours… I thought I might as well make myself useful." When she saw my concerned look she blushed again, "I promise I'll take a nap after this."

We worked in silence for some time, with me just helping set the food out on the largest table in the mess hall, and setting out plates. Truthfully, I wasn't much of a cook either. I filled pitchers with water and with some kind of protein drink the guys had been supplied in the cells; something which I suspected they needed to maintain their impressive muscle mass.

At some point Tori looked at me, licking her lips, and opening her mouth but then she ducked away again. It was clear she wanted to say something but was too shy to say it outright. After she'd done a run-up for the third time I took pity on her. "Come on, I won't bite your head off. Just say what you want to say, girl."

She gave me a wide-eyed look but then squared her shoulders, "It's uh… I noticed last night that that big scaly guy was giving you a lot of attention. Aren't you scared? I mean, I get that you had to share his cell and spend time with him but now we're free right. Why is he still bothering you?"

I stared at her, wow, poor girl had probably been worrying about this all night. Did she really think I was scared of Ziame? That the gentle giant would ever force himself on someone? I felt a little fired up just thinking about that and was about to angrily jump to his defense when I saw how Tori was biting her lip so hard the poor thing had gone completely white.

Grabbing her hand, and feeling oddly motherly when I did so, I started out in the most gentle tone I could muster. "Listen to me, Tori. One," I held up a finger, "Never feel like you can't speak your mind. If you are worried you can always ask and I'll try to keep an open mind."

As she nodded I was relieved to see her letting go of her abused lip and taking a deep breath. I held up a second finger, "Two, we all voted Ziame Captain, including you. Did you just vote with the rest because you felt you had no choice or did some part of you trust him to make the right decisions?"

She closed her brown eyes, face going pale again before she shrugged. "I didn't know if anyone else would make a better captain. They all look so scary to me." I felt a little impatient then, hadn't these men fought for us? Had any of them laid a hand on her? *No, they had not.* The only bad apple had been Geramor and I'd taken care of that bastard.

But I forced myself to look at it from her perspective; painfully shy Tori with her angelic voice. She was thrust into this world just like I had been but she was barely twenty, and pregnant to boot. All these aliens looked terrifying and while I had been an active participant in this escape, she'd just been along for the ride. Through Ziame, I had an easy in with the males, I'd exchanged words with all of them. Tori barely even spoke to me.

"Okay, I get that," I said, "But listen to me. These males were slaves, captives just like we were and they were held for years. Sunder even decades. They are not the bad guys and they have done all they could to keep us safe and out of harm's way. If any of them make you feel uncomfortable it might very well be because they didn't realize they are. Come to me and *tell* me about it okay and I'll sort it out."

She nodded and seemed relieved and for a moment she and I worked together to plate the last of the fake green bacon and get everything situated on the table. When we returned to the kitchen to clean up our mess she worked up the courage to come back to her original point. "But what about you and the big scary green guy?"

It was clear from her question that she didn't even know his name and that everything about Ziame intimidated her.

And what about him really? I told him I wanted to try dating when we were both free and I stood by that decision. A part of me did struggle with how completely alien he was, even compared to some of the other gladiators.

Then I shrugged at her, "Any of Ziame's advances are welcome and I trust him. If I say no he'd back off immediately." Seeing the doubtful look on her face I explained, "I woke up from stasis four nights ago and was thrown into his cell for the sole purpose of getting pregnant. The Krektar thought he was just a beast and he'd fuck me if he had the chance. Guess what he did?"

Tori stared at me with wide, shocked eyes and I couldn't help but compare her to a little fawn. "He made sure he stayed well away from me on the other side of the cell and when I fell asleep he sat next to the bed just to keep me warm. He never touched me and even when they activated his pain collar he'd make sure I was safe. We spent a lot of time in that cell talking, did you know his species is matriarchal? He's used to deferring to the ladies. Sunder too. If you firmly tell them something they'll probably get right on that."

That last bit made her giggle while she clearly tried to picture it and when she, blushing furiously, said: "So if I tell the big guy I want fancy boots like yours he'd find me some?" She pointed at my ugly footwear and then eyed her soft ballet flats and giggled adorably again.

Tori was just… So small and cute and delicate and still far too thin looking to appear healthy with her big pregnant belly. On earth I might have been jealous of her tiny height, I felt distinctly not feminine a lot of the time when I compared myself to my fellow women. I'd sadly dated enough jerks to know that earth men often were intimidated by my height too.

With the way Ziame called me little female (and compared to his eight-foot height I really was) a lot of those ruffled feathers had been soothed. Now I could see how much this made Tori feel insecure and scared, how these men were giants to her of frightening proportions. I mean even *I* had a foot on her, she barely reached up to the nipples of the smallest male aboard. I was actually happy I wasn't a little smaller.

When the first male came in he paused in shock, staring at the spread table. "Is this for breakfast?" Fierce asked in a hushed tone of voice, staring at the eggs and fake bacon and licking his lips. Tori and I shared a look and I finally saw something click in her head, she nodded at me and then with a deep blush approached the table and quietly started explaining to the poor guy what we'd (mostly Tori) made.

ఌ

Ziame

She wore the shoes and she even came up and thanked me for them. When she willingly sat at my side during breakfast I realized it wasn't just wishful thinking, she meant what she'd said in the cell, and she hadn't changed her mind. It had my chest all aglow the rest of the morning while the other gladiators and I trained in the gym.

We hated leaving the females and Luka to deal with more of the cleaning chores without us but we needed to be in top form when we fought for ourselves on Xio in three days. We couldn't afford to miss out on training. Still, Sunder set us up to work and talked us through our training schedules like usual but then he joined the females as they worked on cleaning the bridge and some of the hallways.

In the gym, Jakar raised another problem, "What about our transcoder, and call sign? Drameil knows the details of this ship, when we put in on Xio that's alright but as soon as we arrive in another port it'll be an issue. By then he'll be looking for us and he'll be furious."

We tossed out ideas while we sparred and worked out. In the end, we knew we'd have to get our hands (illegally) on a different call sign and transponder. This meant finding a wreck of a similar class ship but in a pinch, we could probably do with any as long as we weren't in visual range. That would at least work while in space itself.

"A problem to work on the moment we leave Xio?" asked Thorin. "We need to focus on getting the credits for the fights or the gold or whatever bartered goods Drameil arranged. Right?" That was definitely a hurdle we'd first need to take, I was not very familiar with the money end of things regarding gladiator fights but I knew someone who was. "I guess we need to have a chat with Thonklad," I said.

Later that day I found Abigail in one of the hallways of the upper deck, the four of them had made good progress with the clean-up and I felt guilty that I hadn't been helping out. Abigail immediately shot down that notion, "No, you guys are training so you can risk your damn lives to earn us money, that's far more important than cleaning some hallways and rooms. It's not as if I have much skill to bring to the table otherwise." She'd added the last with a rueful smile and I'd bristled though I didn't know how to make her feel better.

In the end, I'd discussed the financial worries with her too and she'd brightened, "If I knew how to read this damn alien script I could take care of that. I'm great with numbers." Impressed I'd set about solving at least that issue, well aware that most ships could display any language in the database.

When I showed it to her after the evening meal she teared up. Clutching her hand over her mouth she trembled and just when I was about to start panicking that I'd really fucked this up she leaped at me. I caught her and we tumbled into the captain's chair with her straddling my lap. "Thank you Ziame," she murmured, and then she pressed her face into my throat and nuzzled, just like a real Lacerten kiss.

Her breath on my scales made me groan and I tried hard to reign that shit in, this wasn't about sex. She was just grateful I'd made something easier for her, that I'd made it possible for her to work on our finances from her end because that was her skill. Except, my body didn't get the memo, readying for her at just that sweet touch like I was a damn teen who couldn't control his first erection.

She brushed against me and this time a low moan did leave my throat and she looked up, startled from her perch in my lap. "Oh..." she said, dark eyes wide in that face so dark and soft looking with those long black lashes and that cloud of beautiful wild curls. I couldn't read the expression on her face, maybe it was too alien to me for that, but she didn't move away and I sure could read the scent in the air.

When I flicked out my tongue and tasted the pheromones dancing between us I groaned again; she wanted me. This wasn't wishful thinking on my part. "Abigail," I mumbled at her, sliding my palms over the delicate arch of her spine, one up and one down. Until I held the back of her neck in one hand and the sweet, so sweet, curve of her tailless behind in the other.

Her eyes turned wicked in that temptress's face and then she pressed herself against me, riding the straining evidence of my arousal with the V between her legs. My eyes rolled into the back of my head at the sensation and then instinct took over.

ʚɞ

Abigail

Whew, who knew he'd be packing that much heat? I thought as I shamelessly pressed against him and then I had to giggle internally. Okay okay, given how big he was, it was no surprise he was big all over. *Obviously.*

Maybe it was rash, maybe it was crazy but I really really liked this guy and I wasn't going to hold back. Not right now when I was free to make my own choices after days of angst, not when in another few days Ziame was going to risk his life on the arena sands just to make money for all of us.

So when he suddenly picked me up and spun around, pressing me down into the chair, I didn't protest. When he proceeded to nuzzle my face and nibble at my ear I moaned out loud. The next thing I felt was his hand press between my legs and another cup my breast and... *No hang on*, that was his tail between my legs because he was holding *both* my boobs. I groaned at the stimulation.

"Abigail," he murmured and nuzzled his face into the valley between my breasts, the gold of the ring through his nose warm to the touch. "Let me see you," he said, his voice so growly I almost couldn't understand. "Please?"

When I nodded he carefully picked his way through the tiny buttons that held my blouse closed and with each inch of skin exposed he leaned forward to nuzzle and flick his tongue. I felt so sensitive, so hot that I couldn't breathe, nothing had ever been this sexy. All I could do was hold on to those horns of his and mutter encouragement.

My shirt and jacket were pressed open soon enough and then he was licking along the edges of my pink bra, making appreciative noises. The tip of his tail was still pressed against my core, rubbing softly with maddening pressure. This guy was far too handy with that thing.

Then he flicked one of the cups of my bra down, tucking it under my breast, and focused that tongue on the straining peak. I groaned, *oh split tongue,* I had totally forgotten but hallelujah that was good! I almost came then and there when he tugged on the stiff peak with the damn thing.

"Ziame, please!" I didn't even know what I was begging for at this point. More? Less? Did I want to have sex with him in the damn captain's chair? It would sure as hell be one way to christen the ship ours but for our first time?

He took any coherent thoughts right out of my head though when his tail finally picked up the pace. Rubbing against me just right while his tongue and fingers played with my breasts, I exploded, moaning his name, my spine arching. "Shit, that was good..."

When he lifted his head it was to grin at me smugly, "Liked that did you, my sweet Abigail?" I could only nod at him, far too sated for the moment to care about the male arrogance he was displaying when he smirked like that. Then he melted my heart when he leaned in and nuzzled his face against my belly, "You have the prettiest skin. Such a beautiful dark shade, so deep and soft and tasty looking; I want to lick you all over."

And then he set my panties on fire, no wait, I wasn't wearing any.

CHAPTER 11

Abigail

"My cabin or your cabin?" I asked him when it became evident he was content to simply nuzzle his face against my belly and not pick up and continue the sexy play he'd initiated. When he raised his head his green eyes nearly glowed and his ears were perked up further than I'd ever seen them. It was very cute.

Up close I could see a soft muted green dot right at the start of the spiny mohawk on his skull. Curious, because it looked entirely different from the rest of his scales I brushed a gentle finger against it. He shivered, "Don't poke at that sweet," he said and then he started tucking the lapels of my jacket closed around my torso.

"What is it?" I asked, momentarily derailed from my quest for actual sex with the big guy. His body fascinated me, it was so very very different. It excited me in naughty, illicit ways, and I wanted to know everything about it. Explore him.

"My third eye," he said and then he swung me into his arms and started off the bridge. I clutched at his massive shoulders, tilting my head back to look at him, my heart racing in my throat. I had never been carried around as much as I had with Ziame, he really *was* making me feel dainty.

Then his words penetrated fully. *Woah, a third eye?* He literally had a third eye. *Sure why not?* "Really? It looks nothing like your other eyes." This was much more like a discolored scale, there was no iris, no pupil, and it clearly couldn't move.

He shrugged and winked, "It's only for sensing thermal images and light levels. It helps me detect danger from above." Wow… this guy was just built for battle, wasn't he? So many different weapons or protections, what was his planet like that he'd developed all of this? I probably didn't want to know.

When it didn't take him long to reach a door I hadn't been through before, I realized he'd taken me to his own cabin. It was larger than the one I had and was fairly close to the bridge. Gazing at the king-sized bed with the neatly folded blankets at the foot, I could see why he'd chosen to go here. Though the bed was bolted away from the wall a little, the placement looked odd.

Then I was sailing through the air and landing with a soft

bounce on the mattress and I didn't care about the location of the bed. "My cabin," Ziame growled and then he tugged my boots off my feet and prowled up my body with the hungriest stare I'd seen on him yet. His tail for once not touching me but swishing through the air behind him, betraying his excitement.

He placed one knee on each side of my hips and leaned on his knuckles beside my face, his large horned head looming over me. The position was dominant and possessive, but his eyes were gentle when he searched mine, "Are you good with this little one? Tell me no and I will stop."

I searched my mind for a moment but I couldn't think of a single objection. I was still slick between my legs from my earlier orgasm. So I reached up to stroke my fingers over the pretty emerald tracings on his long ears. Watched as he shivered when I gripped his horns to pull him closer so I could nuzzle at his throat. "Yes."

He peeled apart my shirt and jacket and helped me shrug out of them, then he went to work on my bra, and impatiently I shimmied out of my pants. When I did that he raised his head and groaned, long and deep, his eyes focusing on the black curls at the apex of my thighs. His forked tongue slid out to flick at the air.

The next moment he slid down my body and ran that tongue straight through my slit. It had me shouting in surprise, my spine curving off the mattress. "Crap Ziame! Warn a girl!"

He raised his head slightly and raised one nubbed brow in question, "Should I stop?" The question was asked with a devious smirk curling his lips and I felt an answering flutter deep in my belly.

"God no!" I shot back and had the pleasure of hearing him chuckle as he nuzzled the inside of my thigh. I wanted more of that, much more. That had been far too quick and sudden for me to fully appreciate just how good that felt.

"Good, I plan to be here a while, you taste so sweet." He bent his head, making a place for himself between my thighs, and got down to business. My eyes rolled into the back of my head as he lapped at my sensitive flesh, learning and discovering just what made me tick.

When he found the right rhythm he got me close to that edge several times, always backing off and nuzzling at me before starting right up again. After the third time I was so excited and so frustrated that I was wildly tugging on his horns just to keep him there a little longer, so I could finally hurtle over the edge.

He worked a finger into my tight passage next, just one but it was thick and ribbed from his scales and when he curled it just right, working in tandem with his talented tongue I finally found nirvana. I screamed, I'd never screamed like that before but I didn't care. I saw stars and I swear that was the longest, hardest orgasm of my life.

I sank down from that cloud of bliss slowly, my legs clutched tight against his cheeks, hands still curled around his horns. When I opened my eyes to look at him I saw he'd raised his head enough to watch my face. At the eye contact, he licked his lips with that wicked tongue before darting it out and lapping slowly at my engorged clit.

Just like that I came undone again.

ග

Ziame

Watching Abigail come was the most beautiful and sexy thing I'd ever seen. Her taste was far better than anything I'd ever tasted, I could probably stay between her pretty thighs all night but after her fourth orgasm, she begged me to stop. Her flesh was tender and sensitive and she wanted to cuddle. I liked cuddling too so I prowled up her body and curved her naked, sweaty body against my chest. "Sleep then sweet, so I can do that again, soon."

She smacked a palm half-heartedly against my pec and laughed, "You're insatiable, I've created a monster." If it weren't for the soft expression on her face and the laughter I would have gotten worried but it was clear she liked this. Then she pressed herself even closer, curling into me and her soft thigh brushed against my trapped cock. I saw stars and couldn't hold back the hiss rising from my throat. I wanted her so badly, my dick was so hard it almost hurt but tonight was not the night; I needed to be patient.

Abigail however stiffened and then pulled away, sitting up. "Oh, I'm so selfish. You haven't come yet!" Her eyes were wide as she let them roam over my tense body. I couldn't help but preen just a little under the look, which heated as she watched me.

I liked that she wanted to be fair to me, but this was a gift for her, and I didn't want her to feel obligated. I had to make sure she understood that so I waved a hand at her and then gestured it down my body, delighting in the way her eyes tracked the movement. "It is alright, not tonight. Not until you are certain you wish me for your mate."

Her eyebrows went up, those pretty black curves over her dark skin, and deep brown eyes. I loved how expressive they were, especially when she thought I couldn't see in the dark. "What mate thing?" she asked.

Oh, of course, she wouldn't know about Lacerten mating practices, nobody but one of my own kind would. I felt so comfortable with Abigail that it was hard to remember that sometimes. It was difficult to think with my cock hard and her naked body kneeling at my side too but for her, I tried.

"I am almost certain my mating drive will engage should we have intercourse." That was good, that sounded steady and calm, keep it clinical so it didn't show how it made me nervous to talk to her about it when she wouldn't be feeling the same drive. "If it does, I'll imprint on you forever. It's like..." I scrambled to remember the human word for mating I'd learned in my anthropology classes on her species. "Marriage? Only as you're not Lacerten it'll engage on my side but it won't bind you."

Her mouth dropped open and then her eyes skimmed down my body again to rest on the erection tenting my loincloth. "Are you saying that if we have sex, you'll be biologically married to me? But I won't be to you? And you don't want to get stuck?"

Horrified at the way she'd worded that I shook my head and scrambled to explain. "I do want to be mated to you!" I started out with and when that made her lean back from me I tried to dial down the intensity a little. "But you don't feel the same drive so we should take it slow so you have the chance to find out if that's what you want too."

"And if we don't there's a chance you're stuck on me while

I could walk away later, it would be another kind of slavery to you." She said what I hadn't even wanted to consider but she was saying it with a softer look in her eyes. As it was nothing but the truth, I forced myself to nod.

She eyed me again, more contemplative this time, and then her eyes came to rest on my erection, which kicked hard at the attention. I groaned, "Stop that. Please, I'm hanging on by a thread here. Maybe you should head to your cabin Abigail, so you can think about this."

But she was shaking her head hard now, "And leave you like this? Hell no. How's that fair to you?" I raised my brows, ears perking up and I sternly told myself that she wasn't offering to mate with me now. Abigail clearly had something else in mind because she spread her legs a little as she shifted and then gestured at my cloth-covered cock. "Let me see it Ziame."

I groaned but obeyed, tugging the fabric away so I was bared to her. She hissed in a breath and then reached out a hand tentatively. "Can I touch?" she asked, voice husky and when I nodded she ran a finger from the base of my shaft all the way to the tip. "Looks almost human in shape. Just the tiny scales give it a bit of texture. Never mind all those pretty little lines decorating it."

My eyes were riveted on the contrast of her dark skin as she curled her fingers around the much paler green of my cock. Then she applied just the right pressure as she rode that hand all the way to the tip and I hissed, my eyes rolling back into my head. "Good?" she asked and I could actually hear the smile in her voice.

At my nod, she added a second hand and started a slow rhythm that drove me crazy but wasn't enough to bring me to completion. I watched her face as she worked me, flicked my tongue at the air when I sensed her own arousal rise again, she liked doing this. With a hand, I reached out and slid it between her slightly spread legs and she moaned when I thumbed her clit. "Ziame," she said and she sounded like she was reprimanding me but at the same time, she was pressing herself against my fingers.

I laughed, "You like this." Then I lost all sense when she leaned forward and darted out her pink tongue, running it across the head of my dick. "Gods!" I groaned, at the molten heat that shot up my spine and tightened my balls. "What are you doing?"

She lifted her head to look at me with a mischievous smile, "What, you've never received head before?" When I shook my head with wide, startled eyes her eyebrows climbed up. "Never?" she asked and then contemplated my cock head again with what looked like confusion. "No one's ever wanted the worship this beautiful thing?"

I opened my mouth and flicked my tongue against my fangs, "Lacerten females have these too you know. We're venomous as well as capable of breathing fire… Not something you want to uh… receive head from?" She eyed my mouth again and then looked down at her own crotch and raised an eyebrow. "That's different," I defended, "I don't actually put you *in* my mouth, I just licked you… No risk of fangs."

She laughed, "I believe you but it seems unfair and unlike your females, I don't have fangs." She flicked her tongue against her blunt little teeth, mirroring what I'd done, followed by a wide grin as she eyed my cock again. The greed in those eyes made it twitch and my mouth water, she really wanted to taste me; *never in my wildest dreams.*

Leaning in, she licked the head again, and then with a saucy smirk she wrapped her lips around it, engulfing the sensitive tip entirely. With a hoarse shout, my hips came off the bed, *that felt so good!* She pulled back and wiped her wrist over her mouth and grimaced, and guiltily I realized I'd nearly choked her with that move. "I'm sorry I didn't mean to do that."

She gave a sunny smile, "Are you kidding me? That was sexy and you taste fantastic. Just try to hold still now that you know what to expect. Can you do that?" I nodded quickly, anything to get her to suck my dick at this point, holy crap that was good.

As she went back to work I focused hard on keeping my ass planted on the bed and after a while it was easier to focus on how she sucked me in a rhythm, bobbing her head, and working me with her hands in tandem. It was nothing like sinking into a warm cunt but damn if that suction wasn't one of the best things I'd ever felt.

Her slick arousal coated the air, her pheromones tingling across my tongue, and with my fingers, I tried to work her clit in tandem with how she worked my cock. I imagined that's what it be like when we actually mated and the thought of sinking into her ratcheted up my arousal another notch.

Then I remembered my tail and unwound it from her ankle, sliding it up her thigh so I could press the tip against her drenched opening. We both groaned at the same time, *shit she felt so good on my cock and my tail.* She raised her head for a moment and said with a moan, "Damn Ziame, that's so good."

Taking it as permission I softly pressed the nubbed, prehensile tip of my tail inside of her; working her with it in a steady movement while flicking her little clit with my finger. In turn, she focused on my cock and it wasn't long before we were both panting, close to the edge.

"Going to come little one," I tried to warn but she ducked down, hollowing her cheeks and when I shouted hoarsely with my release she swallowed every single drop. I only had to work her with my tail and fingers a few seconds longer and she followed me over the edge; collapsing forward to rest her head on my thigh, right next to my spent cock.

"I have no words," I told her after a long silence. When she gave a beatific smile from where she lay but didn't move I shifted my arms and tail, releasing it from the tight grip of her sheath. She groaned in protest but then snuggled down eagerly when I tucked her into my body, her head on my chest. She fell asleep within moments and with a deep, deep sense of contentment, I followed her soon after.

CHAPTER 12

Abigail

We were approaching Xio, only ten minutes until we'd break through the atmosphere. Already, Ziame had spoken to ground control and we were good for the approach. I didn't know exactly how it all worked but it sounded somewhat similar to how an airfield with normal planes might work on earth. Except that flights weren't planned so much as that you'd just request a landing slot on arrival.

The past three days had been strange but good in many ways. The gladiators planned to fight on Xio had worked out hard to hone their skills, usually doing so for several hours in the morning and one or two more in the evening. The rest of the time those with no other important skills worked at getting the ship as clean as possible

Sunder and Tori had taken it upon themselves to do an inventory of the ship's hold but that was a massive undertaking as it was more than half-filled with what were likely stolen goods. Until we got more knowledge on what things were worth, it wouldn't be helpful to try and offload any of that. Though I certainly hoped we'd earn a pretty penny that way eventually.

The inventory was so massive and confusing that Tori had complained twice already that she'd lost something she thought she'd already counted. A crate of rations and a smaller box of dehydrated breadcakes of some kind. I figured that might be pregnancy brain talking though. It was already confusing to me to take a single step into that hold and Tori still couldn't find her way anywhere, getting completely turned around the moment she stepped into a corridor.

Kitan was thankfully on the mend, that is to say, he was out of the woods and currently confined to bed rest, which he did not do graciously. Sunder spent time with him though, making sure they hammered out the details required for hiring a good navigator. He was well enough to make an appearance on the bridge and set the autopilot correctly once they'd taken off and he'd insisted on being helped to the bridge to take care of our landing.

I was fairly certain that Ziame was relieved about that because otherwise, he'd be the only one qualified enough to make the attempt. I think he'd been envisioning our fiery death upon landing vividly all day until Kitan had announced he'd do it.

"Everyone's got a com on them right?" I asked for what

was probably the tenth time that hour alone. We'd found a good amount of those, a lucky stroke as the box that contained them had been right near the door to the hold. Sunder and Luka knew enough to configure them and had handed them out. We'd each be able to reach each other anywhere on the ship or the planet as long as the ship was in orbit.

I absolutely hated the thought that I wasn't going to be allowed to go down to the arena even though I probably would hate every second of watching my friends fight. That's what they'd become over the days though, fast friends, not to mention Ziame whose cabin I'd shared since that night.

Right now, the plan was for Sunder, as a free male, to head down to the spaceport's bars to scout for a navigator. While Ziame, Jakar, Fierce, and Thorin headed for the arena in one of our small transports. As we wanted to have the Doc on hand in case any of them got hurt, he was to pose as their handler while the ones fighting wore fake pain collars.

Ziame, who was still in the captain's chair while he surveyed Sunder and a propped-up Kitan at the helm, gave out a low chuckle. "Of course Abigail. Luka has his right there on his shirt and Sunder's got his too. You know none of the fighting males can have one."

Luka was hovering over Kitan's shoulder as he worked on our landing one-handed, as the other arm was still in a cast. It had been badly broken two days before the fight, due to the bad training gear and he'd neglected to mention it. Choosing to fight through it, was according to him, the only reason the damn Krektar had gotten the better of him.

"You can stay here with Kitan, ready to fire up the ship, and you can watch the fight on the viewscreen should you want to." The censure in that voice told me he probably preferred I didn't watch him fight. I wasn't sure I wanted to either but at the same time, not knowing how it was going might very well be worse.

The landing went off without a hitch and I left Kitan alone on the bridge to see them all off in the hangar bay. Ziame was going to be flying the shuttle that would take them to the arena and they'd drop off Sunder along the way. I half expected Tori to be there too but she was a no-show, maybe she was resting as I knew she'd been up again early that morning. She and Sunder had been spending a lot of time together though so I had expected her to say goodbye to him.

The other males all boarded the shuttle, Luka dressed in the best clothing we could find, looked very nervous as he did so. Ziame waited at the door, turning to look at me with an unreadable expression on his face. "Don't worry too much alright? I have much to return to." When I felt my eyes actually tear up a little at the thought of him being in two back-to-back three-on-one fights in not too long he hurried to pull me in his arms.

"Look, you did really well renegotiating the terms of the fight with the organizers. You hammered out the details of payment, earning us even more than before and you arranged for the payout to happen here so it goes to us instead of Drameil. You did an amazing job. Now let me do my part."

I had done all that, didn't mean I liked any of this, even if I was the dumb-ass that suggested it in the first place. Grabbing hold of his horns I tugged his head down so I could look him in the eye, "You come back okay. I can't do this without you."

I'd been independent all my life, I'd also been alone. I knew I didn't want that now, not out here in space where everything was scary and strange and dangerous. I wanted Ziame so he needed to come back and then he needed to be true to his word and never ever do this again.

"I promise my sweet," he said, deadly serious, his long ears perked straight forward to show his attention was fully on me. Then he leaned in and nuzzled my face, the smooth band of his gold nose ring warm against my cheek.

When he let go of me, he walked into the small shuttle with his back straight but his tail clung to me as long as it could. From inside the shuttle, I could see three pairs of eyes on me, probably on our entire exchange, the only gladiator who'd kept his peepers to himself had been Sunder.

The door slid shut and I backed up so that the shuttle could leave. I tried hard to make myself feel amused by the younger gladiators and their curiosity. It was better to focus on that than on Ziame heading for what seemed to me impossible fights. *Come on Abby,* the others all thought he could do this, it should be alright.

ೞ

Ziame

"Sated your curiosity?" I asked the other three fighting today and was gratified to see them guiltily snap upright. They knew they shouldn't have been looking at that private moment, but they had anyway.

Jakar shrugged, shaking off my censure like it was water, but Fierce frowned after a moment and shook his head, "She chooses you? She's your mate?" It was clear he couldn't wrap his head around the entire concept. For a moment it felt as though he thought I was unworthy of a female like Abigail but then I realized it wasn't that. Sunder and Kitan had both been something before they'd been forced to be gladiators, they'd had lives of their own. Though Sunder's was half a lifetime ago.

Fierce on the other hand had always been a slave, sent into gladiator training at fourteen and fighting ever since. That life was all he knew. Of course he wondered about relationships and how those worked, he'd probably never seen healthy examples.

"She has not yet chosen to be my mate," I said gently because I didn't want to lie. "But I will try very hard to convince her." I winked and that made them lose their stiffness and chuckle with me. Fierce and Jakar shared a look, but when I settled my eyes on Thorin, his darted away.

"I wish you luck then," said Jakar, he looked thoughtful, a little envious even. The young Pretorian male clearly wanted a mate of his own; I couldn't fault him for that. I was far too elated and happy to know that out here in the Zeta Quadrant I'd finally found a female of my own.

Finishing my pre-flight check I sent us out of the hangar bay and started weaving us through the spaceport until we found the right bar. According to our galactic database searches, this bar on Xio was one of the hotspots for navigators, finding one here should be easy for Sunder.

The older male was dressed in a generic jumpsuit, the kind we'd found dozens of in all of the ship's cabins. We'd had to change the back panel to accommodate his wings but thankfully Luka had been handy with some needle and thread. A belt around his middle was weighed down with a gun and a blaster and his com was clipped to his lapel.

Before we reached the bar he went around with each of the males and discussed some last pointers for the fights. Weaknesses, things to watch for, and tells to cover. He saved me for last, just as I touched down in a nearby parking lot. To me, all he said was, "Good luck. I have faith in you."

Once he'd left, the air in the shuttle became far more subdued. Luka was just one big bundle of nerves, he was posing as our handler, and he had to collect the payment. He was obviously afraid he'd give the game away and get us all trapped in slavery again. Us gladiators, we were far more familiar with our current roles, instead sinking into standard pre-fight rituals.

As I set our shuttle down in the assigned spot I turned on my companions, my brothers. "We can do this. Once this is over we'll have credits, we'll have freedom, and we can go where we want to go." Trading handshakes we all saved Luka for last instinctively. Turning on the male, the four of us all at once, looked at where he'd been observing us from his seat.

"Brother," I said to him and watched his eerie black eyes grow more reflective. Grabbing his slender hand I hauled him to his feet and tugged him into a proper clasp. Fist around wrist, "You can do this. Pretend you're in a play, or you're back home, or maybe just pretend you're the Caratoa's captain. Just know, I trust you and we'll have your back."

"Aye!" chorused my fellow gladiators and Luka nodded, squaring his shoulders. "I can do this as long you all do your damn hardest to come out of that arena alive." He met the eyes of each of my brothers over my shoulder and then lastly rested them on me, "Especially you. I can't bring your body home to Abby. I can't. So you damn well survive."

Grinning I shook him a little, "I'm counting on it." But in my hearts, I knew a back-to-back fight was going to test me to my limits. I was just as likely to get seriously hurt, die, or come out the victor. I did know that I had never, in all three of my years as a gladiator for Drameil, had as much to fight for as I had now.

When the shuttle door opened I showed nothing of my turmoil, hiding what I felt behind my beastly facade as always. As I'd always made sure to be too wild, too uncontrollable, Drameil had taken to putting a lead to my nose ring. As I slapped the lead into Luka's hand he visibly swallowed, struggling to hide his distaste but then his mask slid into place as well.

Luka led the way with a disinterested look on his face, leading me on that damned lead like he was walking a pet, and not a very well-liked one at that. The other three gladiators walked at our heels, supposedly kept in check by virtue of their pain collars.

We were ushered into the bowels of the stadium, through the back doors and unvarnished, of despair-smelling tunnels, that housed the fighting stock for now. While Luka spoke with one of the fight's organizers to check where we would be housed for the afternoon, I spent a moment looking around. Checking out the competition waiting in small cubicles in this narrow corridor.

I'd been on Xio several times before, not that that meant I knew much of the planet, as all I'd seen was the inside of a transport and the arena. But I knew the layout here, down below, and I knew how things would go from here on out, what to expect. That at least settled my nerves.

They dropped me off first, unlike the other three who'd just sit on a bench in an open cubicle. They stuck me in one of the cages usually reserved for the non-sentient beasts they also pitted out on the sands. Like the Ferai beast still locked in our old cellblock with only the stinking Thonklad for company.

I paced the cell back and forth in three steps, walking in a groove that many feet had followed before me. I focused on the fight ahead, on the first three opponents I knew I'd face. In my head I recounted their statistics over and over again, making sure I remembered their strengths and weaknesses.

Xio's primary arena, the Dome, was not as large as many of the arenas I had fought in. It was meant for the very elite only, so tickets went at a premium. Each of the fighters pitted on its sands was a prime fighter, having had far more wins than losses under their belt. Generally, fighters of the prime class won more than seventy percent of all their matches, and once that number started dropping they were sent in for death matches, like Sunder.

Knowing this, I knew the stands would be filled only with the richest and most privileged. I'd fought many prime fights because I'd never been defeated at all. The fact that these organizers were now allowed to pit me in two back-to-back fights, three against one, probably had everyone salivating.

All these rich assholes would want to be the ones to personally witness the Beast's first defeat. Fierce, whose hearing was the best out of all of us, had whispered to me that the betting odds on my second fight were 39 to 1 that I'd win. I fervently hoped Abigail didn't hear about this.

The other three all went out on the sands, one after the

other returning victorious. While Luka paced in front of my cell or watched from the handler's bench near the entrance to the sands. I couldn't tell the male to settle down and calm down lest he betrayed us to the organizer watching him with interest. The Beast wasn't supposed to be able to talk at all.

As the headliner for this night of fights, I was the last one scheduled to go out there. When the announcer started prepping the audience for my first fight it felt like forever and then some had passed. I wanted to get this over with, there was only so much warming up of my muscles I could do to prepare for this fight inside this tiny cell.

When I stepped out on the sand everything felt so damn familiar that for a moment I could hardly remember that I fought a free male this time. I was fighting so that Abigail and the others, so that I myself, could live our lives as free people. That was a worthy cause.

Luka unsnapped the chain from my nose ring and whispered at me, "You can do this. Try to keep your back to the sinking sun, I noticed it's particularly bright this sunset." That was good advice that I hadn't expected from the Doc. Keeping my back to that sun would ensure my opponents had that bright light straight in their faces, blinding them.

Barefoot I walked across the warm sand, reaching the middle and raising my arms high in the sky so I could roar for the audience. It whipped them up in a frenzy, they were screaming my name, applauding. Ironic that they cheered me on when each of them had bet that I'd lose my second fight tonight. Of course, these fights weren't meant to the death but it was not uncommon for one or two causalities to fall on such an evening regardless.

Then my first three competitors entered the arena and the

fight was on.

ꟹ

Abigail

When I returned to the bridge I found Tori awkwardly perched on one of the jump seats at the back wall of the bridge. As far away from Kitan as possible and Kitan was just as awkwardly sitting in the pilot's chair, the tension between them thick enough to cut.

Eyeing the two I said, "What?" My eyebrow raised in inquiry, and I pinned each of them with a stare. Kitan rolled one shoulder, dipping his head with the pointed fox-like snout, and refused to meet my eyes. Tori however met my stare but her face turned completely scarlet. "Come on, spill it you two," I asked, hoping this would provide me with a distraction so I wouldn't think of Ziame risking himself.

Eventually, Tori whispered, "The baby kicked, I let Kitan feel it..." And now they were both feeling awkward, how interesting. I wasn't sure if there was attraction brewing between the two or if this was just them being awkward over the tender moment.

Either way, it wasn't a distraction at all. I just rolled my eyes and sat down in the captain's chair, my leg jittery with nerves. Kitan gave me a sideways look and then very carefully said, "Shall I put the match up on the viewscreen? They won't have started yet. Probably another hour or two before Ziame is up."

I shrugged, trying to act nonchalant, "Put it up when it starts I guess." Then I eyed Tori again, "Do you know who fed the beast and the prisoners today?" I knew that Fierce was usually the one to do it, but the males had been too busy prepping for their fights this morning.

She hesitated a moment, the red in her face had gone and now she looked a little sick. "I went with Sunder. His cage really needs to be cleaned but we don't know how to go about it… They normally would knock him out with the pain collar but we think that's cruel."

"Shit yeah, that's really cruel indeed. Maybe Luka can sedate it?" I offered. Then another thought crossed my mind, "In zoos don't they usually have the ability to isolate an animal in one part of their cage? Maybe when we sedate it we can make a sliding door between two cells? So for next time, we can just lure it to one side with food?"

"That is a great idea female," Kitan said, "We should do that. I know Jakar is handy enough with some tools, he can probably make such a thing." He grinned widely, a foxy grin that displayed all his sharp, glittering teeth.

"We really should find a safe planet to leave that poor animal on, keeping it on the ship is no way to live," I added. Wondering if I needed to make sure the males understood that or if they'd like to keep the dangerous animal as a pet or something. I couldn't imagine Ziame wanting to but he had told me this animal was normally kept as a pet, not that I could see how.

"Of course," Kitan said, "He has lost his bonded, there is no way to safely keep it now." He agreed with me with a solemn nod and then eyed Tori who was still perched in her jump seat. She looked away, red tinging her cheeks again and I noticed how that made Kitan's grin even bigger.

She looked awkward and now ventured to softly ask, "What about Sunder? Is his mission going alright?" We had worried that Sunder might be recognized in one of the bars when he tried to procure us a navigator and found us a lead on a replacement transponder so we could change our ship's identity.

He'd been advertised for today's fights as one of the main contenders, as his fight had been the only death match on the docket he'd drawn a crowd. Except, now it was canceled and replaced with Ziame's impossible twofer. Kitan couldn't do it himself, he needed to be here to fly the ship and was still too hurt to go out, so Sunder it was.

I eyed the fox-like male for a second, wondering if Tori's concern for Sunder bothered him in any way. The male was trying to scratch beneath the cast on his arm with one of his claws and was clearly frustrated it wasn't working. There was no apparent interest in Tori's question except when he casually mentioned he could send the Tarkan male a message.

Tori nodded anxiously, she was nibbling on her lower lip, and I realized maybe I was wrong about her being interested in Kitan. Maybe she was interested in Sunder, she had been spending an awful lot of time with him. Then I shook my head, don't be stupid, this could just purely be friendship, it wasn't like Tori was in a good place to look for a boyfriend.

In many ways, I reminded myself, I wasn't either. I had after all just been abducted and thrown into this crazy world, I could hardly trust my own feelings now could I? I thought of Ziame risking his life today and felt cold fear clench my belly and crawl up my throat. I remembered only too well how it felt to lie curled up in his arms each night, I wanted him back safe and sound, I wanted him at my side.

My thoughts were interrupted when Sunder's face appeared on the large center viewscreen on the bridge. He was wearing a billed cap on top of his head that covered the crown of short horns he sported and his slate-gray eyes were worried. The tusks that stuck up from the bottom of his mouth were more pronounced in this face-only shot, ten times enlarged on the screen. From the corner of my eye, I saw how Tori winced back, clearly disconcerted by the close-up of the gargoyle male. No wonder, as he really was rather ugly and scary looking.

"What's wrong?" Sunder demanded in a hushed tone of voice, "I was just about to enter the bar. Did something happen to Tori?" He hadn't seen her then, lurking in the back of the bridge, his eyes were focused completely on Kitan.

The fox male winced as he shifted his battered body, then tried for a nonchalant shrug, "Just checking in. Making sure you know what to look for." He tried to stretch out a leg and winced again, the smattering of burns that covered him were clearly starting to hurt more. I knew he had another dose of painkiller waiting for him but it was still too early for that.

Luka hadn't protested about Kitan landing us and flying us out of here, he was our only choice after all. But I knew better than the others that if the situation were ideal, Kitan would have stayed in bed for at least another two days.

Sunder growled, "I know what to do. Don't worry. I'll get us a navigator." "A good one!" Kitan interjected and Sunder narrowed his eyes, "I'll get us one who'll get us away from here and you can sort out the rest. We can't be picky right now." The connection broke right after and I heard Kitan curse and growl under his breath though he didn't try to call back Sunder.

I turned to check if Tori was at least reassured and discovered the girl had slipped off the bridge without a word.

Which left me alone with my thoughts and an irritable male while I waited for news on Ziame's fight.

CHAPTER 13

Abigail

Kitan had put the fights up on the screen the moment they started. I'd watched through my fingers as Jakar fought and won and then a while later when Fierce did the same. Kitan cheered openly and shouted instructions or insults as if he was simply watching a football game; it was a little unsettling to be honest.

It was barbaric and far worse than simply watching an MMA match on tv. For one, these guys were actually equipped with weapons, at least Fierce had been wielding an axe and shield and his opponent a net and spear. Jakar had thankfully fought unarmed against an unarmed male.

Kitan explained that the unarmed fights were the warm-up for the more action-packed weapon fights but it had looked extremely brutal to me regardless. I was certain Jakar wasn't seeing straight out of one eye and had a broken arm even though he'd actually won. With his four arms that seemed like the most likely outcome in a wrestling match though, no wonder his opponent had played dirty. Never mind Fierce who'd taken several jabs and cuts before he'd managed to get his adversary disarmed and tapping out.

Then there was the actual arena which actually looked like how I'd expected it. Like a sci-fi version of a coliseum, with metal and stone seating in a circle around a big expanse of sand. Fancy seating boxes separated the rich, from the less rich crowd, and vendors hawked food and drink. The crowd itself was made up of hundreds of different species, some I recognized as similar to the males on the ship, many completely strange.

Most prevalent was a species that looked covered in feathers, bipedal but with raptor-like legs and winged arms with clawed hands at their tips. They had maws with sharp teeth, a long feathered tail, and an impressive variety of feathered crests on the heads of what I suspected were the males. They looked like raptors with opposable thumbs, though they came across as fairly fragile and slender compared to many of the other species.

When I asked, Kitan explained they were called Xionians and that the tropical planet Xio we had landed on was their home. The Xionians were a versatile race that had managed to remain a separate entity, holding off annexation from more powerful nations near their space. Mostly they'd done so by being a good place for relaxation for the rich; having enough natural resources to sustain themselves but not become interesting to their neighbors.

"Oh Thorin's fight is starting," Kitan warned me and I sat up a little straighter to watch. Already raising my hands to my face in case I needed to cover my eyes, I hated it when the violence became bloody. "Is Ziame fighting with weapons?" I asked as I watched Thorin strut onto the sand as if without a single care.

He was kitted out in a leather kilt of some kind, composed of many thick strips of leather hanging vertically from a wide belt. Vambraces covered his forearms but otherwise, he wore nothing else. For weapons, he was only wielding a single long knife and a slightly longer, curved sword. His opponent was dressed the same but he had a shield and a sword, it hardly seemed a fair match.

Kitan chuckled as if I'd asked a dumb question but his entire posture was strained, he was in a lot of pain. "Ziame is always armed, but no, no additional weapons. His opponents will all use the weapon they're most comfortable with." Shit... How was he fighting goons with swords when he had nothing to deflect them with? That sounded extremely risky and dangerous. Why had he ever agreed to this? *This was crazy.*

Possibly sensing my spiraling thoughts Kitan eyed me and said almost gently, "Look, he has knives all over his back and tucked against his arms. He can hold his own. Now watch Thorin, he's almost ready to finish the fight." I tried to see what he'd seen as I eyed the screen where Thorin and his opponent were circling each other, each dripping blood from various cuts. What made him say Thorin was winning? It looked like they were equally wounded.

Then Thorin made some kind of whirling fast move that had the other male's shield spinning through the air. The sword swirled around his curved blade and then spun away in another direction. With a final decisive spin, Thorin kicked his opponent in the head and it was lights out for the big guy. I stared in utter shock, I had no idea the male could move that fast. Had he been holding back all along?

At my surprised look, Kitan chuckled again and then he groaned and clutched at his midriff with his right arm, the one without a cast. "Yeah, Thorin tends to play with his opponent. He thinks it's fun and the crowd likes it." Then he shook his head, "Dumbass."

I shook my head, it had certainly looked like Thorin had enjoyed that fight, I could see why the crowd was going wild. Maybe not the safest thing to do though, prolong a fight, when anything could go wrong at any moment. I really hoped that Ziame wasn't the type to do such a thing but honestly, I doubted it. He was so levelheaded and down to earth. For a guy pretending to be a raging beast for near on three years, he was actually pretty calm and composed, a thinker.

There were another two fights between Thorin and Ziame's bouts so I had to sit tight a little longer. Just as the first fight was finishing up there was a sound and then Sunder's face showed up on the viewscreen. "Got a nav, coming in through the backdoor as we caught some unwanted attention," he said and I could see he was running over the space dock, ducking around ships and stacked crates. I wasn't able to get a good look but it was clear he was running with someone at his side.

"Shit," Kitan muttered, "We can't leave yet. How well can you shake them?" I didn't know which them they were talking about until Sunder turned his com unit a little toward the sky and I could get a look at several tiny little drones following him. "

What are those?" I asked. But Kitan didn't say anything in response, looking on with narrowed eyes, hands on the controls. They looked like they were just a little rotor to fly and a big bulbous body for a camera. Were they tracking Sunder back to our ship or was it a bigger problem than that?

"I'm not the best shot," Sunder said with obvious disgust, then he eyed someone at his side for a moment. "How about you?" he asked over his shoulder but whatever the other person said I wasn't able to catch it over the com. Sunder turned his focus back on us, never losing his stride as he ran across the dock. "We'll take care of it. ETA ten minutes."

When the viewscreen turned black Kitan cursed and appeared to struggle with getting to his feet for a moment before giving up and cursing even louder. With a defeated sigh he swiveled to look my way, "Someone needs to go to the small side hatch and let them in manually. Preferably with a gun in hand for backup in case they need it." He gestured at his injured leg and the severe array of sci-fi-looking bandages that covered his chest. "It can't be me."

This left only Tori and me aboard the ship and no way were we sending the pregnant woman into what might be a dangerous situation. "Okay," I said, "Tell me how to get there and what to do. And where can I get a gun?"

Kitan pointed at what looked like a built-in storage locker at the back of the bridge, inside was a neat row of large guns and a few smaller ones on a shelf below it. "Oh, a weapons locker right here?" I said in surprise which netted me the dry response, "This *was* a pirate vessel."

I picked a smaller gun that looked like it would fit in my

hand and then turned to Kitan for a very quick rundown on how it worked. Eyeing him as I did so and noticing how badly he was strained by his injuries at this point, the poor guy should be in bed. "Take the shot now Kitan," I told him and picked up the syringe Luka had prepared. "We need you at your best the next little while, it won't be more than an hour now."

He eyed the thing with what was clearly distaste but then gave a sharp nod, the fox ears on top of his head pinned back all the way. "Okay, go ahead," he said and I wasted no time pressing the injector to his bicep just the way Luka had shown me that morning. "There, now tell me how to get to that airlock."

A few minutes later I was at the door, leaning to one side so I had the best view out of the small window without being seen. On my com, I gently informed Tori that Sunder was inbound with the new nav and that she better stay out of sight. I promised her I'd let her know Sunder was safe and sound the moment I knew but otherwise she agreed to just stay in the mess hall.

I was expecting Sunder and the new guy at any moment and I was anxious to get back to the bridge. I hadn't been sure if I wanted to see Ziame fight but now that the choice might be made for me it didn't feel right. I wanted to know what was going on, wanted to be reassured by the viewscreen that he was still alive.

I leaned a little closer to the small window to get another look at the dock on this side of the ship. It was just a big stretch of tarmac with various spaceships parked all over and stacks of crates waiting to be loaded. The entire place was busy with activity, small floating forklift-like things ferrying crates to and fro, and spaceships coming and going. Then there were the various aliens walking around, it was just one big hive of activity and it was difficult to spot if any of the moving figures in the distance was Sunder or not.

A hard thud on the outside hatch had me jumping back in shock and then suddenly Sunder's fearsome face was peering in through the small window. Heart pounding from fright I hurried to pull the hatch open. I struggled with the heavy weight of the thing, using the manual opening mechanism and not the automatic one like we'd used in the hangar bay of the ship.

As soon as the door started opening Sunder shouldered his way in, then leaned out to pull someone up from the tarmac. A moment later two bags were thrown inside and a woman followed the big gladiator into the small airlock. The two barely spared me a glance but instead both quickly shut the hatch, leaving only a tiny crack, and then they peered out as if checking if they were followed.

"See any?" Sunder rumbled in his low, gravelly voice.

"No, I think we took care of them all. They won't be able to guess which ship we boarded out of the dozens here." The female didn't speak English or any earth language I could recognize, though much to my surprise she looked entirely human. Her hair was a shocking shade of red and her eyes when she finally glanced my way were this beautiful shade of gold. That was definitely *not* human.

When she straightened to her full height I realized she and I were the same size, which was a surprise because I rarely met a girl as tall as me. She cocked her head, red hair sliding over well-shaped. muscular shoulders. This chick was stacked. Wearing a tank top and work pants with scuffed boots, covered by a long leather duster, it was clear she was one tough lady. She looked like she could bench-press *me* if she felt like it.

Still, when she moved to turn toward me and get a good look at me the way I was at her, she moved gracefully, womanly. She might be tough looking and strong but she was all woman, with makeup highlighting her striking eyes and red coating her full lips. She smirked at me, "Well hello there, aren't you a cute one." I had the unsettling feeling that this woman didn't generally think much of other women.

She shrugged her shoulder and then strutted to the airlock exit. "Show me what I've got to work with then, Sunder the supposedly dead one." Another cocky smirk was aimed at Sunder who looked pensive and maybe a little miffed though that was hard to tell since he always looked growly and fierce.

I was about to pass the new nav to point the way to the bridge when Sunder grabbed my arm and held me back. "I've got what we need, Strewn, it's a shipyard two weeks out from here." From the excited tone of his voice, I knew he was happy that he'd managed that part of his task, arguably the hardest part.

"That's fantastic Sunder, I guess we'll be headed that way the moment the others return." As he let go of my arm I gently patted his shoulder, not in the least surprised that, unlike the insides of his palms, the skin there felt pretty much exactly like touching stone, except it was warm.

The tall, red-headed woman behind me scraped her throat in what was obviously annoyance, "Are you guys always this slow?" From the corner of my eye, I saw Sunder glare at her disrespectful attitude and I matched his glare.

"This way," I said and gestured for her to finally head out of the airlock. As we started walking I told the Tarkan male, "Sunder, can you let Tori know you've returned?" At my words, the male brightened considerably and with a nod, he shouldered the two bags our new nav had brought with a little higher, "I'll drop these in your cabin." We split up in the corridor and I led the new female toward the bridge while Sunder headed for the cabins and mess hall.

"Welcome aboard," I said, trying to be friendly when the female was making me a little uncomfortable. She was probably just rough around the edges, a little abrasiveness was to be expected from a woman picking up a job like this on her own. That was risky after all. "I'm Abigail, what can I call you?"

She appraised me again with those sharp gold eyes, "Abigail huh? Human, I presume? Freed slave just like the rest of this lot?" I couldn't tell if there was any judgment in her tone of voice so my spine stiffened, worry curling in my belly. Was this going to be a problem? Did we need to make sure she didn't send out any coms?

Shrugging I said, "What makes you say that?" Striving for nonchalance without confirming what she said was true. But a pit of worry was opening up in my stomach, I should have thought of this problem, we should have prepared for it. Although it wasn't as if we had much choice either, if we wanted to fly anywhere, we needed a navigator.

The woman raised a shoulder to her ear, "I have eyes. And Sunder's face has been plastered on posters all over the city for weeks, announcing his match." Exactly what we'd worried about, so he'd been recognized, at least he'd shaken his tail and gotten us a nav. Though it remained to be seen if we could work with her, she still hadn't given me her name.

When we stepped onto the bridge the female's eyes immediately went to Kitan who was sagged out in the pilot's chair. He straightened with a wince the moment we arrived and then his eyes widened and they stayed locked on our new nav. "Sune," he said in a growl which didn't sound friendly at all.

The female shrugged and acted as if his hostility didn't matter, "So are you." Well, that cleared up the species thing, *not*! The woman looked nothing like Kitan, they couldn't be the same species. But listening to their speech I could vaguely tell that they spoke something that sounded similar even if my translator did all deposit it in my brain as if I had just understood my own native tongue.

My attention was drawn to the viewscreen however because I suddenly saw that Ziame was moving onto the sand. A close-up showed me his fanged mouth as he roared for the public, his spikes standing up straight all over his body. "It's started!" I yelped, rather awkwardly and I felt embarrassed when both Kitan and the newcomer turned to look at me in surprise.

Then the woman popped a hip against the nav console and eyed the viewscreen. "Ah yes, the big fight with the Beast, two back-to-backs I heard, impossible odds." She send a lazy look my way, "Hadn't pegged you for a fan, pretty girl."

I didn't have an answer for a moment, rather insulted and shocked by her demeanor but it was Sunder who'd just stepped onto the bridge who put her in her place. "That's enough Diamed, that's the first mate you're trying to insult there."

The woman, Diamed apparently, straightened and frowned my way, "First mate? Her?" This was the first I heard of it too but I tried to pretend I'd always known that, I figured the males thought I was because Ziame was Captain. *Who knows?*

Pointing at the viewscreen I indicated Ziame, "And that there on the sand is your Captain and you better believe he's coming back." I focused on Kitan, "All the betting closed yet on his fights?" I was suddenly filled with the desire to show how confident I was in his ability to come back. I wasn't about to let this 'Diamed' think I was worried.

He nodded, "They'll open up the betting for a brief window after the first fight. You betting on your male?" When I nodded sharply he grinned with his scary fox-like snout, this big cheeky grin that showed all those sharp teeth. "I think I'll do the same. We'll put all the credits we found in the crew cabins on him yeah?"

"You can do that from here?" I asked, my eyes already focused on Ziame and his first three opponents. They looked fearsome and scary to me but I realized as they neared my male, as the guys here would say, that they were not anywhere near Ziame's size.

Two were the same species, burly and muscled they were red-skinned and covered with intricate swirling marks but otherwise looked human. I'd seen one of their kind before, aboard this ship, the gladiator who'd sadly died in our uprising. These two seemed to be working in tandem, each equipped with a spear and shield as they tried hard to flank Ziame.

The third male was a little bigger and less human-looking. Skin black and cracked looking with deep purple running between the fissures. His head was adorned with two horns, far smaller than Ziame's impressive set but lethal-looking nonetheless. His hair was like a lion's mane, wild and thick and strikingly purple. Clawed hands and feet added another dangerous element and I figured that weird-looking skin was as tough as Ziame's. He held a long blade, a sword much like one of those two-handed medieval things and he wielded it effortlessly as he tried to drive Ziame into the spears of the other two.

"I can do it from here with the creds but if we win big we might need to ask the others to cash us out to gold." Kitan spoke but his words hardly registered, "As long as we can get out of here as soon as possible." I waved my hand at the new addition now sitting at the nav console, her large duster draped over the back of her chair.

Sunder came to stand at my shoulder then, "He's keeping the sun at his back, that's smart." I eyed the fight again, watching how Ziame had managed to keep all three in front of him while he caught a spear thrust on his bladed forearm and twisted, breaking the spear shaft. "Yes!" I cheered but then gasped when that second spear went under his guard and caught him in the side. "No!" Heart pounding I frantically searched for any sign of blood but on his dark green scales, I couldn't tell.

The others on the bridge were talking but I wasn't paying attention now. I was worried too much that Ziame had gotten badly hurt, the fight wasn't supposed to be to the death but those were real weapons. What if these three took their chances and he got fatally injured?

Ziame roared when he took the hit, shook his head with those wicked horns, and then twisted his body just as that large sword came swinging for his head. He ducked just in time, swung his head around to catch one of the red males in the midriff, and with a flick of his head, he flung the male several feet through the air until he landed hard in a heap in the sand.

The male with the still-functioning spear glanced at his fallen comrade but didn't let it distract him further. He rushed in and bashed away Ziame's swinging tail with his shield, jabbing at him with his spear.

Ziame ducked and punched at it but couldn't get in reach of the male himself and didn't manage to repeat the success he'd had with the other spear. Now he'd lost the advantage of the sun too, they'd rotated on the sand so that the sun hit their flanks instead.

I had lost track of the male with the sword but Ziame clearly hadn't. When that male suddenly charged him from behind his tail was ready, catching the blade and spinning it away. While the male was off balance he ducked the other guy's spear, spun around, and charged, hitting the now swordless opponent in the belly with the top of his skull. For a moment I figured Ziame had impaled the guy on his head spikes but when the guy was flung ass-over-teakettle it became clear he'd flattened his spikes at the last moment.

The guy groaned but didn't get up and there was loud cheering from the stands, possibly trying to incite the guy to get back up again. Meanwhile, both red-skinned males had rallied and while one now had a spear without the sharp pointy bit, the two still charged him from behind. One deftly engaged Ziame's tail and the other ducked that still functioning spear under his guard and jabbed him in the hip.

I saw blood this time and whoever was in the editing

room for this broadcast clearly did too because they showed a close-up of the injury, the way red droplets dripped down his leg and fell into the sand. The red males cheered as they backed off, not pressing their advantage but egging on the crowd instead. "Why are they doing that?" I asked and Sunder answered, pressing a reassuring palm to my shoulder.

"The idiots think they have the upper hand. Ziame looks dazed but he's just playing it up. That little nick in his scales? That's nothing to him." I hoped Sunder was right because it sure looked like something to me.

"That's some of his thickest scales," Kitan murmured, "The outsides of his legs and back are the most heavily armored. He's fine." But Ziame favored his other leg when he moved to face his opponents. The black-skinned, horned male had stayed down so far but the other two were cheering and yelling taunts, egging on the audience. When they charged again it looked as if Ziame was off-balance, braced on one leg but when they got within range his tail whipped out, not aiming for the shields but swiping low and catching them in the ankles.

One went down, and the other managed a glancing blow to Ziame's shoulder but it lacked punch. He was tripping and trying to regain his footing. In the distraction, Ziame punched out and hit the tripping male's shield, actually sending him sprawling. Then he was on the other male, batting aside the broken spear, ripping the shield away, and then punching the downed guy hard in the face.

They showed a close-up of that too, showing the way the male's nose broke and blood sprayed. How his eyes rolled into the back of his head as he passed out. It was honestly horrifying how they were so focused on any show of blood.

"Watch your back!" Sunder suddenly urged and then I saw why, the male who'd seemed down had just been biding his time. Now he was up, running for Ziame as he was distracted by the other two. He'd picked up his sword along the way and send it swinging for Ziame's exposed back. Horrified I watched, that was a deadly-looking blow, there seemed zero effort in making that non-lethal.

Ziame rolled just in time off the now unconscious red male and I saw his mouth open, arms coming up for a block with the blades on his forearms. Not fast enough though, not fast enough. My heart was pounding so hard I thought it would burst from my chest.

Fire blew in a stream from Ziame's mouth, engulfing the blade and both of the male's hands where he held the weapon. There was screaming, and a lot of cheering from the stands, but the blade was already in motion. It came down, by sheer luck I imagined, on Ziame's left horn. Then the male was stumbling back, staring horrified at his still sizzling hands.

I figured Ziame would go after him and knock him out but I'd forgotten about the second red-skinned male and he hadn't. He spun on that one instead, the male had just recovered and was moving in on him, but not fast enough. Ziame moved, so quickly his tail blurred. He whipped it round again and wrapped it around the spear, yanking it away, and then he leaped at his opponent.

The two traded blows but it was clear that the other male was no match in sheer brute force compared to Ziame and soon he too bit the dust. When the male passed out after a fierce right hook Ziame spun on the other male with the burned hands but the guy was still on his knees, and the moment they shared a look Ziame's opponent bowed his head, signaling surrender.

In the arena the crowd was going wild, cheering for the Beast who'd just won his first match. On the bridge of our stolen pirate ship, I was quaking in my seat, my legs jelly, and my belly so tied up in knots I couldn't even puke though it felt like I was about to. Ziame was hurt and he had to do this all over again in five minutes, probably less.

He was raising his arms, accepting the adulation of the crowd like it was his due, roaring for effect. Standing tall, he acted like he wasn't hurt at all but I saw it, saw how when he left the arena he limped, still favoring his leg. Saw how just as he entered the exit tunnel he rubbed at his shoulder where he'd taken that glancing blow. He was hurt and he still had to do this again. I couldn't stand it.

Kitan and Sunder were talking as they spoke about placing the bet but to me, it sounded like they were talking underwater. I couldn't believe how quickly Ziame had come to mean the world to me but he had. It was rash and crazy and clearly partly because of our extreme circumstances but I loved him, I did. The revelation itself had me as dazed as my worry for him a moment ago.

I loved him. I needed him to come back to me and there was absolutely nothing I could do from here. I was helpless to stop this second fight, they'd never let him out there. All I could do was wait, pray that he'd survive, and have faith in his skills. Clenching my fists I tried to ignore the stats now displayed on the viewscreen, showing the next three fighters Ziame was about to face. "He's coming back," I whispered to myself, then I said it more firmly out loud.

A hand folded over my shoulder and squeezed hard, Tori

was suddenly at my side, her eyes filled with sympathy. "Yes, he is. Ziame will do anything to come back to you," she said gently. And suddenly I was incredibly grateful the girl was there, so far I'd felt like the big sister, trying to look out for her. Right now, she was there for me though and that mattered far more to me than I thought it would. I'd never had anyone look out for me like that before and now I had Ziame, I had Tori, and a ship full of gladiators.

If they all made it back here that is.

CHAPTER 14

Ziame

The moment I was out of sight I dropped the limp and headed for the bench where Luka was waiting with the other gladiators. They handed me water that I quickly guzzled down and the Doc hurriedly ran his scanner over me, checking both the shoulder and the hip, and making sure to apply some healing gel that sealed the minor cut.

"No deep bruising, you are fine," Luka murmured, then he shot a glance at the guards at the end of the long corridor. There were some other owners of fighting stock as well but most had already left with their winning or losing fighters.

The red Xurtal twins had been revived after they'd been stretchered off the battlefield and they studiously ignored me as their trainer tore into them about all they'd done wrong. A harried-looking medic was treating their bruises and the broken nose I'd given one of them. They would be fine and probably up for another fight the very next day should their owner want to, no serious harm. Didn't sound like they were into too hot waters with the owner either so that was good.

They brought in my third opponent then, he was on a stretcher too because I'd cracked several of his ribs when I headbutted him. I had been shocked to find him on his feet after that and even capable of lifting the claymore. I fingered the slight notch in my horn where the blade had hit as I eyed the Kertinal on the stretcher being carried by.

His purple eyes focused on the movement, pain-filled from the burns covering his hands from the tips of his fingers all the way to his elbows. I'd held back on that breath of fire but that probably was a cold comfort to him. Still, he tipped his chin to me in respect and I found myself even more sorry that I'd hurt him so badly even if it was a life-or-death kind of situation.

"Are you ready for the next round?" Jakar asked, interrupting my thoughts. I eyed him but focused on the Kertinal's progress down the hall until they dropped the stretcher unceremoniously near a wall where his handler was waiting; there was no medic and the handler barely glanced at the male. I had a bad feeling about that but I couldn't afford to lose my focus now, I had another fight to win.

"Some muscle fatigue," I said honestly as I shook out my limbs to stay limber and warm. "No issues from the hits I've taken so far. Hip good Doc?" I asked. I kept my voice pitched low so that only the males I trusted would hear me speak. Wouldn't do to give away the trick this late in the game of course.

"All patched up, should be fine, want a stimulant?" the Doc asked me solicitously and I shook my head. "No, this win needs to be undisputed." As I shared looks with the other gladiators we all knew that such honesty would likely not be followed by the next three fighters I was up against. Their owners could decide to dose them up for better performance. These fights were more often than not rigged so the organizers and owners made big bucks on the betting.

I eyed the Kertinal with the burned hands again, well aware he'd been slated to fight Sunder and win. Before the fight, they'd have shot Sunder up with a drug to make his coordination off, not enough to make the crowd notice, enough to make it a sure win for the other male. The Kertinal's owner would have lost big money by the change in the fighting schedule.

Then the announcer was calling out my name again, my cue to walk back out onto the sands. I shook out my limbs, accepted claps on the shoulders from my brothers, and then set all thoughts of the Kertinal's fate from my thoughts. I couldn't afford distractions now, my mind needed to be on the fight and the fight alone.

Still, as I accepted the adulation of the crowd, raising my arms high and roaring all my thoughts went to my Abigail. I hoped she hadn't been watching the fight on the viewscreen, I didn't want her to see this. If she had been watching, was she now worried because I'd leaned into that limp when I left the arena? I'd played it up to make the next fighters underestimate me but it could well have frightened her.

They announced my opponents, each one receiving even more cheering from the audience than the last and I appraised them as they stepped onto the sands. The Tarkan was the most worrisome, he had flight capabilities and stone skin, which made him hard to hurt. The other two were the Asrai twins Pu'il and Kitan were supposed to fight, as newcomers to the circuit, no one aboard the ship had known what kind of psychic gift the two might have.

With their death-mask markings, they looked terrifying and angry but the serene look in their eyes told me they had mind-linked and would work as a cohesive unit. I needed to watch out for them and with their nictitating membranes, the sun wouldn't bother them nearly as much as it had my previous set of opponents.

I circled anyway, putting my back against the sinking sun, it didn't bother me much either but maybe it would surprise them at some point. At that Drameil, my previous owner had at least worked hard, as I was one of his greatest sources of white-washed money. Many of my less noticeable advantages had been kept hidden, such as my third eye or the membrane.

The Asrai twins were kitted out with a shield and short sword and they worked to protect each other's flanks as we exchanged blows. I caught their swords' swings on my arm blades or with my tail, ducked others, and had to avoid spear jabs from the Tarkan male who'd either jump in at my back or try and swoop in from above with well-timed dives as he spread his big leathery wings for some airlift.

We were at a stalemate, none of us giving ground and I struggled to find an opening to take one out, they worked well as a single unit. Even the Tarkan had found a way to integrate into the duo's fighting style, a testament to his skill as I knew he'd never worked with these two before. They weren't even owned by the same person.

I couldn't sustain combat like this for much longer, muscle fatigue was a serious risk and while I could fight through that kind of pain for some time it wasn't conducive to a good outcome. I needed to take out one of the twins, that would destabilize the entire grouping.

My opening came when I ducked to avoid a spear coming down on me from one of the Tarkan's aerial attacks. Likely the male thought I was more vulnerable from above but my parietal eye gave me ample warning each time. As I ducked the attack I happened to be sweeping my tail around to parry the blades of both twins. It brought my head low and I went into a dive, rolling my entire body underneath the Asrai twin shields.

There was no breath to spare for a gust of flame so I did the next best thing, clamping my fanged mouth around the nearest ankle. I didn't have the best control over the amount of venom I could inject but I tried to keep the dose low, ripping my mouth loose after only a short second. It did the trick though, the Asrai male gave a hoarse shout and stumbled back.

I barely avoided a blow to the head from the other one's shield and then managed to rally to my hands and knees. This was a bad spot to be in, nearly prone on the sand and between the Tarkan and the remaining Asrai. Especially since I still didn't know what kind of psychic gift these two might have.

I caught a sideways blow from the Tarkan's spear to my hip, the same one I'd hurt before which was not a coincidence. This was not a little bump though, this hurt, and I went down again. Knowing I needed to move I rolled, for a moment unaware as to where my opponents were located. I thought the one Asrai was down, for now, but that didn't leave the other one harmless.

Sliding my nictitating membranes over my eyes to protect them from the sand I came up, blades bared. It was a good choice as the Asrai had unleashed their psychic gift, whipping the sand into a dust devil around us. The forces were not enough to bother me much and with my thick scales and the membranes covering my eyes, I was protected from the sting.

I caught movement up above, just a flash of dark and heat from my third eye and I ducked a swipe from the spear, lashing out with my tail and yanking and cutting the shaft till it splintered. Flicking my ears back at the sound of approach from behind I twisted to the side just in time to avoid the stab of a short sword, it glanced across my ribs, managing a thin slice.

Slamming my arm down hard on the blade arm I heard the Asrai male's wrist snap and the blade clattered to the ground. There was a rage-filled howl and then the sand devil died down again. I managed a quick glance around, noting the location of each of them. One Asrai backed away, cradling his broken wrist, the other on his knees on the ground several feet away, eyes clenched in pain as he fought the advance of my venom through his veins.

The Tarkan was swooping above me on his massive leathery wings, broken spear still in hand as he circled to try and decide the best approach. I didn't wait, I picked up the broken spear tip with my tail and transferred it to my dominant hand. Taking aim I launched it at the massive target his wing was, hoping to clip him so he'd have to fight from the ground.

Whether the Asrai had tried to interfere or the Tarkan himself had lightning reflexes I'd never know, but the blade scraped the top of the wing, hurting but not debilitating. The Tarkan came down to engage me with his spear shaft in a series of blows though, wanting to bring the fight to me. While the Asrai with the broken wrist attacked me with his sword, letting it dance through the air with his psychic gift while he remained at a distance.

I needed to end this fight, fast, there had to be a way. I was flagging and while I'd dealt them blows they were fresher than I was and determined to win. I eyed the Tarkan male, flicking my ears toward him, his skin was thicker than mine. Taking a calculated risk I changed the angle of my blows, letting him hit me on the shoulder with that spear shaft, hard enough to make my fingers go numb.

I was under his guard now though and I sliced out with the blades on my forearms, slicing open his chest. Not deep because his stone skin absorbed much of the blow, but enough to make him bleed and bleed a lot.

As the Tarkan staggered back out of range I knew I had to deal with the Asrai quick, the other one was rallying and if they could work in unison again I knew I was done for. I ran, surprising my opponents with a burst of speed, dodging the swinging, floating sword as I went. I was on the weaponless Asrai before he could get his shield up for defense. I tore it from his hand and then landed an uppercut to his chin hard enough to send him flying off his feet. He didn't get up again.

Enraged, the other Asrai let out a bloodcurdling scream, raising his arms and sending both his shield and sword spinning my way. I batted the shield out of the air with my tail by the skin of my teeth but I was too slow to avoid the sword, only managing to slide to the side to avoid a fatal blow. It sank into my already numbed shoulder nearly to the hilt.

Biting back my groan of pain I tried to keep my opponents in focus, I had to win. I knew I had to because I had a feeling these guys might not let me live if they had the chance, I'd terrorized the arena for three years. Killing the Beast would net them a lot of goodwill with their owners.

The Asrai I'd bitten had staggered to his feet, his face contorted in anger as he started my way; likely thinking he could finish me off. The Tarkan had also recovered though he kept one hand pressed to the bloody lacerations covering his chest and belly. I flicked the shield up that lay near me and considered getting to my feet but then gave up on the idea. I would be more steady kneeling and neither opponent was at full strength.

My pierced shoulder rendered the entire arm useless but I made a show of struggling to lift the shield to protect myself with my other arm. The Asrai was grinning viciously and it was only now that I could see that his teeth had been filed into sharp points. He was closest to me and I had a feeling he was about to yank the sword from my body and try to stab me again. He wasn't doing so with his gift which probably meant he couldn't muster up the mental strength to do so; a win for sure.

I waited till the last moment, aware the Tarkan was closing in on me in a flanking position. When the Asrai was in range, grinning as if he could already taste victory, I propelled the shield up, bashing him in the jaw. Unsteady from my venom he went sprawling backward and I finished knocking him out with a hard blow from the tip of my tail.

The Tarkan roared, leaped at me and I threw myself to the side, painfully landing on my impaled shoulder. He landed on me though thankfully not on the blade and I twisted my head sideways hard, knocking my horn into his head. I saw his shocked look a moment before they rolled into the back of his head and he collapsed.

Of course, the heavy fucker landed on me and this time I didn't hold back the angry pain-filled groan. The crowd was deadly quiet and I knew I had to get up, get to my feet right now or the game organizer might try to declare this a damn tie.

With a growl, I heaved the Tarkan off me one-armed, and then I had to dig deep to find the strength to get to my feet. The moment I did, the crowd came out of its stunned silence and started cheering and screaming in celebration. That felt good, familiar, I even felt a surge of pride. I'd beaten the impossible odds and I was alive to return to Abigail.

When the accepted time had passed for me to be declared the winner and receive the customary accolades I staggered toward the exit where my brothers were waiting. I never removed the sword from my shoulder, it was in too deep and I'd likely bleed out without immediate assistance. I could tell this detail was very much loved by the blood-hungry crowd.

The moment I stepped into the dark and much cooler corridor where my friends waited I felt my knees go a little weak but then Fierce was there on one side and Jakar on the other. Thorin, I noted, was absent and only the injured Kertinal from the previous bout was still lying on the stretcher where he'd been left, the handler was gone.

Luka didn't say anything, he'd already pulled out everything he needed and was quickly hooking up an IV bag for fluids. Moments later I'd gotten a shot for the pain and my brain went a bit fuzzy though I certainly remembered how Jakar had struggled to pull the blade out. They worked on stopping the bleeding and patching up the wound quickly but the real fixing would have to happen on the ship. "Where's Thorin?" I blurted out, concerned one of our number was missing.

"He's collecting your female's winnings right now, should be back soon," Luka responded. That sentence made no sense to me and I was too foggy to try to untangle that so I left it. "Purse money?" I asked and Luka gave me an exaggerated sigh and told me to shut up so he could fix me. Amused I said to Jakar and Fierce, "His bedside manner is certainly lacking isn't it?"

I shut up the next moment though because I spotted the organizer heading down the hall with an entourage behind him. Two guards and two slaves carrying a heavy lockbox. The Xionian male was a red-feathered one with a white and black crest on his raptor-like head. He flared it out in distaste as he looked at the mess of blood all over the floor.

Lip curled he said, "The winnings," and gestured at the chest. Jakar hurried to take it as the slaves were about to set it down in the puddle of my blood. The organizer gave Luka a hard and distrusting stare and Luka, to his credit, straightened, curled his lip right back at him, and glared. "There a problem organizer Frrraz't? Would you like to take it up with my boss? Lord Drameil?"

The organizer's feathered crest dropped down and he looked away, then he rolled his head on his long neck and said in a clipped tone of voice. "Of course not. Please see yourself out, I have business to attend to." He walked off, followed by the males with him and just as he left the tunnel we could hear him pick up a com call and start talking in hurried tones. I had a bad feeling about it.

"Let's get out of here fast, tell Thorin to meet us at the shuttle," I said gruffly and then cursed when I couldn't find the strength to get to my feet. Fierce pulled me up by my good arm and then with a cheeky grin hung the IV bag he'd been holding from one of my horns. I couldn't be bothered to feel indignant about that, we needed our hands free. Then we staggered down the corridor towards the exit as fast as I could manage.

I eyed the Kertinal on the floor as we passed and realized his eyes were open, he was alive and in pain and his handler hadn't given him treatment and simply left him behind. "What about him?" I asked no one in particular and saw how the male's pain-filled eyes widened in shock. Whoops, now he realized I could speak.

Fierce and Jakar shared a sad look, "The handler was informed by the owner to leave him. He's been written off." "Okay, so we take him then," I told the guys, "Nobody's going to look for him." That seemed simple and obvious to me but both Jakar and Fierce looked startled as if it hadn't occurred to them that this was even an option.

The Doc sighed but then quickly ran his medical scanner over the male before digging around his pack and jabbing the guy with some pain reliever. "Badly cracked ribs, you can pick him up Fierce just be careful or we're dealing with perforated lungs. I'll prop up the big guy."

Fierce handed me over to Luka, who was slighter but still

strong as he took some of my weight and steadied me from under my good arm. While Fierce was surprisingly gentle as he started to pick up the Kertinal. The big male didn't struggle, instead, with a groan, he shook his head. "Legs are fine," he gasped out. "Just help me up, I'll walk."

It wasn't fast, as Fierce definitely needed to support the winded, injured male. But we made it out of the corridor and started winding our way through the arena's bowels to the exit where our shuttle was parked. We were nearly there too when Thorin caught up to us from behind with a harried look, "Hurry," he said, "I think they've figured it out."

He'd only just spoken when we heard shouting go up from behind us. I chanced a look and saw a contingent of guards on our tail so we made the effort to increase our pace. Thorin had taken off his fake pain collar and added a hooded cloak so he could move in the crowd unrecognized. He'd also procured a blaster from the pack Luka had carried in. Now he covered our retreat with it and then dashed to the front to take care of two guards standing near our shuttle.

I steeled myself then and managed a bit more strength and steadiness, hurrying into the shuttle first and plunking my ass down in the pilot's seat gratefully. Pre-flight checks were not a good idea to skip but I did the bare minimum as I warmed up our engines. Behind me, the others piled in and I heard Jakar and Fierce arm themselves and return fire. "Brace!" I yelled, "We'll take off with the hatch open."

Barely sparing my passengers a glance to make sure they were all holding on tight I set the shuttle into motion. Turning it at the last moment so my brothers could get off another round of covering fire and then I aimed us for the docks and took off.

CHAPTER 15

Abigail

I stared in absolute horror at the viewscreen where they were still showing reruns of the goriest moments of Ziame's last fight. *Some asshole had fucking impaled him!* I was a little faint in the head from seeing that, and then again and again as it was one of the most well-liked moments of the entire fight apparently.

"Shit..." I said and Tori leaned in to hug me tightly against her side. "Luka is right there, you saw him walk off the battlefield, he'll be alright." But my head was buzzing from worry. Then I eyed everyone on the bridge and saw how they were looking at me, with concern and pity. And, in the case of Diamed our new nav; definitely derision.

Straightening my shoulders I sat up and gave her a fierce glare, "Get ready for take-off. I'm going to bet we'll need to leave in a hurry." Kitan gave me a solid nod and put his hands on the controls, initiating pre-flight checks.

At my hand wave, Sunder hurried off to get rid of our three unwanted Krektar guests. We'd all agreed we'd simply leave them behind the moment we left the docks on Xio. It hadn't felt right to execute them and it wasn't like they knew where we were going or that the crime lord wouldn't know we'd been there.

"Everyone who can, strap in," I ordered. Then I checked in with Sunder to verify his progress. As the two injured Kretkar had healed enough, we'd moved them to the cells just like Thonklad and I knew all Sunder had to do was escort them out the nearest door at gunpoint.

"Com from our away party," Kitan said, grabbing my attention when Ziame appeared on the screen. I was infinitely relieved to see him, clearly behind the controls of the small, short-range shuttle they'd taken to the arena. He was sitting upright, a focused expression on his scaly face and a thick white pad of bandaging covered one shoulder.

I made sure to step into view behind Kitan's shoulder, standing in front of the captain's chair. His eyes focused on me immediately, "Abigail, I'm afraid we're coming in hot. You better lift off, we'll dock in the air."

His eyes went to the controls he was working, clearly hard at work steering the small craft. Judging from the way the passengers in the back were being jostled about they were moving rapidly and not in a straight line. "Alright, we're just waiting for Sunder to drop off our unwanted guests."

At that moment my com pinged with a message from

Sunder, letting me know he'd strapped into the nearest jump seat. I sat down myself in the captain's chair, locking the harness in place the way I'd been shown on landing earlier that day. "Everyone secure?" I asked and when the sounds were affirmative I ordered Kitan to take us up. I felt a little silly to be the one giving orders but it was exactly what the Sune male and Diamed our ornery new nav seemed to be expecting.

The ship jolted, engines roaring as we shot into the sky. The forces of our lift-off pressed me hard into the captain's chair, much as they had on entering the atmosphere earlier that day. This wasn't like in the movies, where the ship gracefully floated into the sky, this was much more like a rocket take off and it was *intense.*

Kitan had been talking with traffic control about a take-off slot but we hadn't received one yet. Immediately an alarm went off and control appeared to frantically be ordering us to stand down until clearance, then changing their tune to order us to land as we were being detained. We couldn't have that, I was certain that we had no chance of counting on authorities on Xio to take our side. They'd serve us up to this shadowy, scary figure that Drameil was.

"Are you certain you can reach us in time? That isn't strong enough to leave atmo," Kitan was saying to Ziame, who had left his com channel open. He nodded his big horned head, the image on the viewscreen shaking at what sounded like a blast hitting their craft. "I can do it," he said with confidence.

"Whew, I didn't know you were that good a pilot with small crafts. You pull that off and I'll have you flying this beauty in no time," the Sune male joked at Ziame. The gladiator didn't respond though, clearly focused on flying.

Kitan was steering the ship with calm, practiced moves of his hands and steadily talking to Ziame to coordinate their position. The technical jargon was far too difficult for me to follow but I could clearly pick out the small updates Ziame would give on his distance from us as we climbed to escape Xio's atmosphere.

Diamed drew my attention then, by sharply speaking up, "What's our destination First Mate?" Her hands were scrolling adeptly through the holo display projecting star charts between her and the console. "I can hardly get us out of here if I don't know where you want to go."

Was she being serious? This woman? Hadn't she been right here when I'd discussed Sunder's intel on that shipyard for the new transponder with him? Did she really need a direct order? Maybe she did, maybe I didn't understand the intricacies of space travel.

"The shipyard, Strewn," I told her, I eyed Kitan and then Ziame still on the coms and was gratified to see both of them nod. I really didn't like being in charge, why had Sunder put me in this spot? Didn't it make more sense if he was Ziame's second?

"Alright," Diamed said, "Strewn it is." And then she started moving graceful hands through the star charts, seeing things I couldn't even begin to understand. It wasn't long though before Kitan grunted and said, "Locking in the course, thanks."

Then a shudder ran through the entire ship, rattling my teeth and I yelped, "What the hell was that?" I eyed the only two people on the bridge with me but realized that Kitan was really busy and likely couldn't answer. His snout was pulled into a snarl and his golden eyes were practically glowing, I wasn't certain if he was fiercely happy or furiously angry. Maybe he was both.

Diamed gave me a look, much calmer than I was, and then with a sigh, she eyed the empty consoles around the room. "That was a ship firing at our engines, your pilot managed to dodge but it was close." I was grateful for the explanation and at the same time terrified by it. A ship was shooting at us?

"Fuck," I said and eyed the other consoles the way Diamed was. "What can we do? Fire back? Raise shields?" I dared ask, I wasn't sure if any of those things were possible with this ship but it sounded right.

Kitan spared a moment from his concentrated piloting of our ship, "No weapons, shields are up but barely. Holding at thirty percent. Don't worry, I've got this." Then he sent Ziame a fierce grin on the com screen, "You're almost there, I'm opening the hangar bay door. Can you land that shuttle in there at this speed?"

Ziame had been quiet though it appeared his flying had taken on a less erratic path. They weren't being jostled about any longer in the background as far as I could tell. Maybe because they were close enough now that our ship had become the main target.

My big green guy pulled his face into a fierce grin that seemed to match the one on Kitan's snout. "You bet I can. I've done it before." But then something flickered in his eyes, the reflection of red blinking lights followed by a muted bang. "Shit, one thruster's out, we're losing speed."

I felt my heart thump in my throat, no! What did that mean? Was he not going to be able to make it? We weren't leaving him behind! But I shouldn't have worried, there was a jolt and a shudder and then Kitan declared, "Matching speed brother. Hurry up, we can't maintain this long."

The next few moments I sat clutching the edge of my seat, still pressed tightly into my chair by the g-forces of our fast acceleration. It only eased up slightly because Kitan had slowed us a little, a glance at his console told me he had what looked like some kind of radar display; which showed at least seven different blips. The one in the center had to be us and the nearest, the small one, I hoped to god that was Ziame and the others.

There was no sound indicating we were hit but Kitan cursed and flipped some switches to his left. "Shields are down, direct hit to the generator." That was bad, really really bad... But I had no time to contemplate our possible demise, the next moment there was a shudder running through the ship. Then Ziame was declaring victoriously, "Docked, close doors!" And then our ship seemed to buck once as Kitan let out a kind of ululating yowling sound and pulled hard on the yoke. "Right on time brother!"

Ziame's com winked out and the viewscreen was suddenly filled with what our front sensors picked up, essentially making it look like I was watching out of the front window. Glittering space filled my eyes, black studded with stars and a blue and black striped moon that we were fast approaching. The force on my body was also drastically easing and suddenly seemed to go from holding me down in my seat to me actually starting to float away, held in place by the straps.

"Breaking atmosphere. Ready to engage gravity generator in three, two, one," Kitan counted down. With a flick of his hand, the gravity generator was turned on and I thudded down into my seat. I didn't wait, figuring it safe enough; I was already fighting to undo my safety harness so I could sprint down to the hangar bay and see Ziame.

I heard Diamed say calmly, "Well that was interesting, great flying. Was it me or did your captain have an IV bag dangling from one of his horns?" I shivered, yeah I'd seen that too. I didn't listen to Kitan's response though but instead sprung from my seat the moment I was free. I was about to run out when I realized that I needed to be responsible here too, as long as they thought I was First Mate for some reason.

"Kitan," I said, "As soon as you can engage autopilot please do. Then get your ass to medbay so Luka can check your injuries. That was hard work and you're not healed by a long shot." I waited until the male had focused his golden eyes on my face and given me a sharp nod before I started to turn away but he halted me by calling out my name.

"Our pursuers didn't follow us out of atmo, we're in the clear." He shot a sharp golden look at our new nav and then added, "I'll just call up Sunder so he can give our new addition the tour." He was still sitting up straight but I had a feeling that was purely for Diamed's benefit and not because he wasn't in pain. He'd flown this ship with his arm in a cast and his upper body almost entirely covered by bandages after all.

I left the bridge, hoping Kitan was true to his word and rushed in the direction of the hangar bay.

ശ

Ziame

I allowed myself to slump back in the pilot seat when I'd managed to set the small shuttle down with only a minor scrape along the floor. That had been a close call, I'd made myself sound confident to Kitan and the others but internally I hadn't been nearly as certain I could land the shuttle. At least, not after one of the thrusters had gone out, we hadn't just lost speed because if it, we'd lost maneuverability too.

Eyeing the nearly empty, swaying IV bag dangling from my horn I huffed out a tired breath. My shoulder ached, one arm was entirely numb and my ribs were creaking in protest with every move I made. Not to mention the fact that my muscles never did get the chance to properly cool down and I'd worked them hard, every part of me was sore.

None of that really mattered though, *we'd pulled it off!* I'd survived my two bouts of combat and each of us had returned victorious. We'd made a lot of money today, enough for a good amount of supplies and some repairs. It was all starting to look up.

Luka was at my side then, having managed to extract himself from his seat. Honestly, with how my arm was, I didn't think I could undo my own straps though I flicked my tail around to jab at the release button. "Let me," the doctor said calmly and he undid the harness, helping me shrug out of it. "Fierce, help him up please?" he then asked and I wanted to growl that I didn't need help. Except I *really* did.

Letting the gladiator pull me out of the damn pilot chair

felt embarrassing but the male grinned at me, "Holy crap that was impressive brother! I had no idea you could fly like that." Well, that certainly eased my ruffled scales.

He propped himself under my good arm and helped turn me so we could make our way out of the small craft. Passing Jakar I saw how the male was now carefully pressing his broken upper arm against his chest with one of his lower arms while he helped the Kertinal male to his feet. The newcomer was swaying, eyes unfocused as he was clearly in a lot of pain after the rough flight.

Thorin eyed the precious box with our winnings and the sack with Abigail's betting money but in the end, simply left them where they'd landed and went to support the Kertinal on his other side. Then we started our slow and careful way out of the hangar bay and toward medical.

Luka carefully monitored both the Kertinal and myself with every plodding step we took. I was tired enough that I was letting my tail drag along the floor behind me, something I never did; it was simply too much effort to keep it off the ground.

Then I caught Abigail's scent on the air with my tongue and my ears perked forward; I could hear someone running. She came around the corner in a sprint, her long slender legs eating up the space between us. She didn't pause, didn't hesitate despite my blood-soaked appearance. Simply flung her arms around my middle and held on tight, her momentum causing me to stagger though thankfully Fierce braced us in time and helped to keep me on my feet.

"Hmmph," came out as my breath was knocked from my lungs. "Ziame!" was all she said as she pressed her face into my scales. As Fierce was holding me up by my good arm, all

I had was my tired tail to curl around her and I did that gladly. "I'm alright," I said into her cloud of curls, briefly pressing my nose into them and inhaling her scent.

"Shit," she muttered as she pulled away slightly and eyed the blood-soaked bandage on my shoulder. "Oh no, did I hurt you?" I snorted at her, "As if you could little one." Abigail grinned at me and would have hugged me again but Luka intervened, "We need to get to medbay before this big guy falls flat on his face. I doubt we'd be able to easily get him moved once he goes down so I rather not test the theory."

The skin around my Abigail's dark eyes tightened with worry but I gave her a reassuring grin, "Not gonna happen Doc." But I started a shuffle forward anyway because I really did want to get to medbay. Abigail immediately slid to the side, curling an arm around my middle to walk with me, maybe she thought she could help prop me up like Fierce was doing. I was warmed by her concern and her caring.

We made it to the medbay where I was helped onto the medical cot with the surgical arm. I felt bad for the Kertinal I'd hurt with my fire breath but he didn't complain as he was helped to lie down on the other cot to wait his turn. Possibly he was so out of it from the pain by now that he was barely aware of what was going on around him. He certainly didn't speak much.

Luka got to work on my shoulder and Abigail never left my side, holding onto my good hand tightly the entire time the surgical arm worked on me. With more appropriate pain relief administered I could finally relax and find a modicum of peace. "According to my database, you heal fast, correct?" Luka asked me as he finished applying new bandaging.

When I nodded Abigail exhaled in relief, "Thank you, I was so worried. He's going to be fine?" I hated that this was making her worry, but I was eating up the attention too. I hadn't felt this cared for in a long time, I just wanted to keep hold of it.

"He is," I told her firmly, "I've had far worse." Then when that only seemed to agitate her more I added more helpfully, "Two days and I'll be good as new." Her eyes widened and she turned to Luka and only when he gave her a nod to confirm it did she relax. It was giving me all kinds of hopeful thoughts; Abigail was a caring person of course she'd be worried about any of the males. But I dared hope that this meant she felt something much stronger for me.

Now she eyed the freshly stitched-up and bandaged injury on my shoulder and then the work Luka was doing on the minor cut to my hip. He'd thankfully already used the tissue stimulator on my abused ribs to help ease the battering they'd taken. "So how soon are you fit enough to make our mating official?"

My fire starter clicked in my throat in shock, there was no oxygen to ignite though as I'd completely stalled for breath. On the other cot, the clicking sound had made the Kertinal flinch but the rest of the males in medbay had fallen completely silent, staring at our exchange. As they were all injured to varying degrees they'd sat down on the floor out of the way to await their own turn and Tori was going around with refreshments.

"My Abigail," I murmured when I gazed at her earnest eyes hovering near my face. "Are you certain?" I didn't want her to be stuck with me, I wanted her to love me. To be with me because she couldn't bear to be apart from me; the way I felt about her. After what she'd been through she deserved a happy life, and so did I.

She smiled at me, reaching out a hand to gently stroke my ear, it flicked into her hand eagerly. "Yes," she said firmly and I realized her eyes were luminous with unshed tears. "I love you, you big green lunkhead. You're not getting rid of me now." Then she leaned into me and nuzzled her face against my throat in a Lacerten kiss and for a moment every single ache and pain disappeared; my world narrowed down to the female that had taken my heart with her strange stilts and wild hair and her beautiful mind.

"I love you too Abigail," I said and managed to lift my damaged arm to curl it around her slender shoulders. With my good one, I started to push up so I could get to my feet. There was cheering and applause, the gladiators stamping their feet in celebration. Luka was frantically trying to get me to lie back down even though he was fighting a smile.

I managed to get upright, holding my female to me as I got off the cot on surprisingly steady feet. "Treat the Kertinal please Doc," I told him, "And the rest of this lot." I swept my tail around to indicate the others gathered just as Sunder stepped into the medbay, which meant everyone but the new recruit was now in this space; the Doc probably didn't like that.

"Fine! But get some rest Ziame, you're not invincible," the Doc conceded while he initiated the controls on the medical cots to switch them around so he could get his new patient under the surgical arm.

Sunder eyed the crowd, then the male that Luka was now fussing over, and hissed out. "Doom? You brought the male here, that was supposed to kill me?" The celebratory mood dissipated and everyone turned to stare at the male in question in surprise. We'd known that of course but somehow in the chaos of the fight, I at least had totally forgotten. Yeah, this was Doom, the male scheduled to fight Sunder until I'd taken his place.

The Kertinal was getting shots from Luka, pain relief easing his features and with his purple glowing eyes, he settled on Sunder, a slow sigh sawing out of his battered lungs. "Oh, how the tables turned…" then he blinked and passed out, possibly medically assisted by Luka.

Kitan broke the silence, "Well. When's the party? Can we make a cake?" When everyone gaped at him he elaborated, "For the mating celebration?"

CHAPTER 16

Abigail

The males in medbay all cheered for us as Ziame tucked me under his arm and started escorting me to our quarters. If my skin wasn't so dark they probably would have been able to see my blush. Still, I held my head high and smiled hugely at them. A week ago non of them would have been able to laugh and tease like this.

We walked slowly through the empty hallways to the captain's quarters on the top level of the ship. As it was near the bridge and the medbay was located at the center of the ship, we had a ways to go. It was hard on Ziame, despite his bluster and his treatment by the doctor he wasn't in any shape to do anything but sleep.

As soon as we reached our quarters I helped him wash up and then curl up in bed. I left only for a short while to grab us dinner but he was already out like a light by the time I returned. Placing the food next to him on the nightstand I ate what I wanted and left the rest for him for when he woke. Then I undressed and curled up against his side and allowed my body to relax, letting the stress from the past day slide away and carry me under.

When I woke up, it was to the feel of Ziame's warm scales pressed against my bare skin. His warm breath ghosted over my throat as he nuzzled against the skin there. I went from sleepy to horny in the span of moments when I felt a big, textured hand curl around my breast. The tip of his tail trailed up my leg, stroking the sensitive skin at the back of my knee, tickling the inside of my thigh.

"Mmmm good morning," I husked out, laughing when that earned me a flick of his ear against my lips. It tickled and delighted me, I loved how different his body was from mine, and how expressive he could be with it. "Are you feeling better?"

There was a soft growling sound and then he lifted his head to focus his emerald eyes on mine. "Less talking, more mating," he told me but then he wiggled his mobile ears, clearly trying to be funny and I just had to laugh.

When my laughter died down he propped himself up on one arm, the stark white patch of bandaging visible on his opposite shoulder. "I am alright. The sleep did wonders and so did the food." Which had to mean; I rolled my head to eye the nightstand. Yup, he'd found the plate I'd left for him and polished it off down to the last crumb.

Still, that sword had gone straight through his shoulder. If

I closed my eyes I still saw the reruns of that image. "I know you said you heal fast but I'd feel better if Luka checked…" He interrupted me by licking at my lips, then nibbling on the bottom one and nuzzling his way down my jawline and into my throat. Goosebumps broke out all over my body and I immediately lost track of what I was thinking.

"I am fine," he repeated, confusing me for a second, my lust-filled brain catching on a moment later when he sat up straight on his haunches at my side and demonstrated his range of movement with his injured shoulder. "Sore but alright. Bruising is all gone already." His emerald eyes held mine for a long moment, completely serious. "I promised this was the only gladiator fight I'd ever do as a free male. You'll never have to see that again."

I'm a tough girl, I told myself that regularly but this time my eyes filled up. "I was so scared you wouldn't come back to me," I heard myself say in a terribly fragile-sounding voice. Irritated by that, I sat up, so my knees were tucked in between Ziame's big thighs where he sat in front of me. "I know it's unlikely I'd ever be able to go home… But even if I could, I wouldn't want to anymore Ziame. I want to be with you."

There, that came out far more confident, even if my heart was pounding in my throat. I'd just blurted out that I loved him, that I wanted to be his mate, right there in the medbay earlier but that didn't mean declaring myself felt any less scary now. This was a huge decision and our future was still far from certain, even if the universe was huge and Drameil would have a hard time finding us.

He cupped my face in his big palms, managing to make my six-foot-tall ass feel tiny since he loomed over me like the giant that he was. His eyes were tender, "Good, I love you, Abigail." "And I love you, I know it's fast but… It feels right." His declaration was making me feel all warm inside, I didn't even care a lick that I was having this conversation with him butt naked.

"You should know though…" he said, tail flicking forward to curl around my waist. "Earth as you know it, that's unreachable. You were in that stasis pod for a very, very long time." I had suspected that all along, there had to have been a reason Tori and I had been yanked from faulty pods bought on the cheap. A gamble. This explained it.

"How long do you think?" I asked quietly, I felt sad inside but also kind of relieved. I had nothing to go back to on Earth, I'd mourn coffee and chocolate probably. Not to mention my shoe-shopping addiction but those seemed small in the grand scheme of things. Not like Tori who was desperately missing her big Italian family.

"Between two and three centuries ago, before Earth became spacefaring, it was very common practice to nab humans from Earth. So much so that it's not uncommon to still find stasis pods like yours. There's a return to Earth program for such people… We can see if Tori would like that."

Huh, well that was interesting. It was sort of nice to know Earth had made it out of its own solar system, that we as humans were still around alive and kicking two centuries later. Sad to think so many people had been stolen from my planet that a program like that was a thing.

"I'm sorry little one, I know how hard it is to lose your home," Ziame offered, his tail hugging me a little tighter. He did, his home had been lost to him for three years, but he could return to it now. Was that where we would go? Once we were mated? Or were we going to stay aboard this ship and help the other gladiators? I asked him what he wanted and to my surprise, he shook his head. "I can't go back, I don't know how."

It was obvious from his voice that this was bothering him. "How can you not know how to get back?" I asked. He shrugged his uninjured shoulder, "I don't know the coordinates. My ship's AI would know but the ship is programmed to self-destruct if I don't return within the specified time frame. I didn't so it's gone."

I remembered how he'd explained his species was super-advanced but also extremely secular. Their planet was carefully hidden so that no intrepid explorer would ever find it. I understood better now that this meant that Ziame wouldn't be able to return to it either.

"I'm sorry Ziame, you must miss your family a lot," I offered, and to my surprise, he now grinned at me. "It's alright, explorers like myself are only picked because we have no ties holding us back. I found my family, it's right here," he pulled me to him as he spoke until I straddled his big thighs. His mouth found mine, nibbling, and licking and I let the feelings he evoked wash away our conversation.

Raising my hands I curled them around his horns for balance, leaning into his touch, rubbing my face into his throat when he let me. He smelled so good, so warm and safe. I was so lucky to have been thrown into his cell of all people, to find someone like him out here.

He leaned forward, pressing my back into the mattress and coming down on top of me. As always he was careful to keep his weight off of me, just enough to feel him right there, but never enough to feel smothered.

"I love your breasts, so soft and round," he murmured as he moved down my body to nuzzle at them. Split tongue flicking out to lick one of the stiff peaks. Instantly, heat shot through my body, a sharp pang of desire tightening my pelvis. "So tasty," he added in a growl as he switched attention to the other one. His tail had a mind of its own, sliding up my leg and steadily seeking out the slick heat at my core.

My spine curled up on a groan when it flicked against my clit, then slicked lower to press into my passage. I uncurled my clenched fingers from his horns and slid them down his shoulders, marveling at the thick muscles beneath his leathery scales. He was steadily pushing his tail in and out of me, mimicking the act of sex and I was so ready for the real thing. I tried to untangle the knots that held up his loincloth but got nowhere fast.

He chuckled softly and raised himself up from my breasts, the wetness coating the stiff peaks chilling them. My eyes caught on the gold bars piercing his own nipples, distracting me enough that I didn't watch as he worked his loincloth off his hips. With a curious finger, I flicked against one of the bars and was rewarded with a hiss. "Do that again," he said with a growl, his tail stilling between my legs.

I sat up, found his other nipple with my mouth, and nibbled while I flicked the first one again with my thumb. The small gold bar was warm against my tongue. He shivered, his fire-starter clicking in his throat but I wasn't scared for even a moment that he'd hurt me.

He was done playing the next moment, his big hands gripping me around the waist to toss me back into the mattress. His mouth came down between my thighs with a growling, primal sound. "Just a quick taste," he muttered as he licked. Finding the right spot immediately, he'd already figured me out thoroughly with our earlier explorations and now played me expertly.

There was no hair to grab hold of, only sharp spikes that he'd flattened against his skull, but his horns made fantastic handlebars. When I felt myself getting close I held him tight, not allowing him to back away as he'd done before. Thankfully, this time he didn't tease, instead he let me fall off the edge just as he pressed a thick finger inside of me, curling it just right.

"Ziame…" I moaned my legs dropping open from their clutched position against his jaw. Limp from satisfaction. He shifted, prowled up my body, and used his hands to palm my bottom, lifting me up. "Are you ready for me?" he asked, ears perked forward, "You still want this?"

I let my gaze slide down his strained expression, over his muscled chest and defined abs to where his thick cock was straining towards me. *Yes, please.* That needed to be in me as soon as possible, it was going to feel so good. But he wasn't just asking that, he wanted to know I understood this was it, he would never let me go after this. This was the ultimate commitment to him.

"Do it. I want you," I said. Letting him know how much I meant that by pressing my hips up towards him, hooking my heels into his firm behind. He growled, his green eyes flashing while he flexed his grip on my ass to hold me still. "Do *not* move."

When I froze he gripped his cock with one hand and lined us up. I felt the heat of him against my private flesh and couldn't hold back a whimper. Then he was pressing into me, the broad head stretching me with a slight burn until the head slipped past the tight muscle. I made some kind of strangled sound and when he paused what he was doing to check on me I clenched around him on purpose, enjoying the hiss that drew out of him.

"Move, I can take you," I told him firmly. My eyes were glued to the sight of his cock where he stretched me open; only the head was in and I wanted him all. He re-positioned, leaning over me, and then he pressed in, not stopping until he was fully seated. When he was, he came down on his fists over me, bracketing my shoulders, and started to move.

Each push of his hips sent a jolt of heat through my core. His cock was textured just right, the scales and veins causing the perfect kind of friction. And then he brought his tail into play, the agile tip finding my clit and stroking. It wasn't long before my orgasm crashed through me. I may, or may not have screamed his name at that point. I didn't care.

ꟸ

Ziame

Abigail was absolutely perfect as she pulsed around me. I drew out her pleasure as long as I could, struggling hard to keep myself from following her at that moment. I wanted to see her come again, wanted her to unravel and scream my name.

"Again," I told her, telling myself to hold out a little longer. Increasing my pace I leaned down to lick at her perfect, soft little breasts until she came undone around me once more. This time I allowed myself to find my own release. Growling out her name as my seed filled her.

I ignored the twinges of pain in my shoulder when I curled my arms around her and rolled us over; carefully making sure we didn't separate. I wanted to spend forever in this moment with her. She pressed her sweaty cheek against my chest, limp and spent and satisfied. Her dark skin gleamed and her wild curly hair brushed against my chin just the way I liked.

For a long while, we said nothing and I let my mind drift in the feel of her against me and dreams of tomorrow. It wasn't so bad a future, living aboard this ship with my Abigail and my gladiator brothers. Maybe I was more tired than I thought though because it wasn't long before I fell asleep again.

CHAPTER 17

Abigail

Our flight to Strewn would take us a good two weeks and Tori and Sunder had reassured us that we had enough supplies to last us the journey. I cringed a little internally each time thinking about how that might not have been a possibility. How I could have recklessly caused us to starve by saying we'd head for Strewn. I resolved to always be on top of all these details from now on.

To the gladiators and the others I'd officially declared I'd rather be the quartermaster than the first mate and that we should all take a vote on who that should be. I'd then personally nominated Sunder and not a single person had objected, (Tori had voted very enthusiastically this time). I was infinitely relieved to have that burden off my shoulders.

We'd been a day into our journey when the com call came in. We'd spent all morning in our quarters, making love several times and resting in between. I couldn't complain even though I did worry that Ziame wasn't resting enough.

He was still injured, still wearing a bandage around his shoulder, but except for a new notch in his horn, there were no other marks of his fight left. We'd headed for the bridge after lunch (at which we'd been greeted with lots and lots of catcalls) to work with Diamed to figure out a planet to head to next. One where we could safely release the poor mind-broken Ferai beast so it could live out its days free.

Sunder was also there as he liked to keep an eye on our new nav to make sure she wasn't up to anything. We'd all agreed that with her sour disposition, she wasn't the best fit and she'd made no effort to mingle with any of us. She'd been downright rude and dismissive to Tori even, so Sunder was feeling extra protective.

So far we'd made a list of five planets that seemed like options but we needed to whittle it down to something that both worked for the beast and was close by our current heading, Strewn. We had money now and I'd worked hard to make sure I understood how currency worked in this strange new galaxy. Still, I had a long way to go to be really good at this; it was a steep learning curve. Since I didn't want the former gladiators to have to fight again, anything to save money was appreciated. At least this ship could siphon hydrogen from stars for fuel so that resource was free (as long as you did it in an unclaimed solar system or didn't get caught doing it apparently).

"There's a call," Sunder said, surprised. He was sprawled

in the chair in front of the com station, working on something small with a knife. Ziame and I had been standing behind Diamed's shoulder where she sat at the nav-station, and we all turned to look at the blinking lights on the console Sunder was waving at.

"Who is it?" Ziame asked, his brows lowered dramatically which I knew meant he was concerned. His tail had tightened around my ankle a little. Sunder shrugged, "Unidentified but it appears long-range, coming from a planet." With reluctance, he eyed Diamed, "Can you trace it?"

She had adopted a bored pose and now raised a sculpted red brow, "Probably, want me to try Captain?" she asked. Her golden eyes were derisive as she looked at Ziame but the moment he turned her way she flinched a little and set her hands to work. Ziame only grunted confirmation, his irritation clear.

"I think this might be coming from planet Ov'Karal," Diamed said after less than a minute. "They're not doing anything to hide their signal. I think they want us to trace it." I didn't know what this planet meant to the gladiators but it was clear from the dark look Sunder and Ziame shared that it meant something. Even Diamed picked up on that as her hands stilled and she eyed both males. "Say… Isn't that said to be Drameil's favorite place of residence?"

Oh shit… Of course it was. I felt my stomach drop at the simple mention of that crimelord's name. I'd never met the asshole and he didn't even know I existed but I had plenty of reason to fear and loathe him. For Sunder and Ziame that feeling had to be much stronger. I'd heard the story of how that asshole had used Ziame's nose ring to degrade him, walking him like a pet.

"It is," Ziame said, then he turned to Sunder and gave a sharp nod, "Can you mask our location? Surely the pirates had some tech installed to make that easy?" Sunder eyed the console a little apprehensively but started scrolling through options on the screen. It took long, several minutes, where Ziame and I tensely waited, but eventually Sunder thought he had it.

The call was still incoming, apparently this was nothing like how it worked on short-range calls. It was completely normal for a long-range caller to expect huge delays in getting picked up and even delays in the call itself. Kind of like how it was for you know, NASA to contact the ISS.

Ziame didn't let Sunder answer the call until he'd released my ankle and carefully made sure I was out of view. Diamed had no problem ducking out of sight herself but I noticed her morbid curiosity, she was waiting for some juicy gossip no doubt. Thank god she was locked out of our long-range com systems, a precaution Kitan and Sunder had taken. Personal com devices didn't work unless you were in range, so inside the ship it worked and ship-to-ship if you were in close range. Ship-to-planet worked only if you were in the solar system, otherwise, the calls needed to go through the ship's systems like this one was.

The male appearing on the big viewscreen when Sunder opened the line was briefly broken up by static. All I saw was shimmering gold and pale skin. Then the image settled and I saw something that could only be described as a throne, though it was made of black stone and austere and stark in its lines.

The male sitting on it was decked out in robes of gold

while his face was a pale round circle above it. The eyes were glowing coals and slits cut through the cheeks on either side in several rows all the way down to a sharp and pointed jawbone. The jawbone was pointed into a black horn that had been capped with gold. There was no nose, it was just a flat space and that was far more disconcerting than the malicious smirk curling away from a needle-filled mouth.

He stared at Ziame for a moment, not moving, though maybe that was the delay. "My Beast… There you are," the male said in sibilant tones. He managed to make those words sound almost like a pet owner talking to their beloved pet. I bristled, wanting to tell this asshole off but at the last moment held back, aware that Ziame hadn't wanted me to be seen by the crimelord.

Maybe Drameil already knew Ziame could talk, though from what I understood from the reports of the arena, that was unlikely. Maybe he didn't know and was masking his surprise at seeing him standing on the bridge as he was.

Ziame had hidden his intelligence well all this time but I knew he was itching to tell the crime lord off; I knew I was. My male crossed his arms over his chest and flared up the spines on his head, "Drameil," he said, "You must be smarting, losing me from your stable. Didn't think your prized beast was smart enough to orchestrate this, did you?" his tone dripped with derision and venom.

There was a few seconds of delay before we could see Drameil's response but when we did I could tell that he was rattled. The evil male had one hell of a poker face, he barely moved at all when he heard Ziame speak so flawlessly. But at his last words, he hissed like a snake. "No one gets away with crossing me. Mark my words, you'll be fighting for me again."

The connection broke after that and the bridge was engulfed in silence.

ෆ

Ziame

I was seething inside, my scales itching but when Abigail tucked her smaller body against mine and held on tight I instantly felt calmer. "Did it feel good to tell him what a big mistake he made with you?" she asked and suddenly I wasn't angry anymore, I was laughing.

"He was certainly shocked wasn't he? I've never seen him so rattled," I told her before eyeing Sunder who went from tense to grinning. "Neither have I, I think he's going to be running in circles, scrambling to find a way to whitewash his money efficiently."

"Just how powerful is he?" Abigail asked, I honestly didn't know but Sunder clearly did. "As far as crime bosses go, he has some clout but he's not the biggest threat out there. There are only so many places he has reach and as long as we avoid those, we're fine."

I felt some tension leave my Abigail's body so I felt compelled to add to that. "The universe is a really, really vast place. He could never locate us unless we broadcast where we are. We are safe." And didn't that feel good to say? It felt good period. We were safe. Out of that asshole's reach where he was left to bluster and make empty threats. Here I was, holding my beautiful female in my arms after we'd mated.

Life was good.

I was a lucky male.

And a few hours later, when we were celebrating our mating in the mess hall I felt like I was flying. Dancing with Abigail in my arms to some tribal-like music Tori had found in the ship's database, the other males around us laughing and talking. A huge, lopsided cake on the table, half demolished at this point.

"I love you, my sweet sweet mate," I told her and she smiled up at me. "And I love you, now come on. Let's eat more cake."

CHAPTER 18

Kitan

My skin itched. The Doc told me I shouldn't risk a shift while injured, that I should be patient and let the bone fractures heal before I put strain on them again. Patience was never my strong suit though which was why I'd ducked into the cargo hold for some privacy to try anyway.

For nearly five years I'd been forced to shift only when my owner felt like it. I'd been forced to fight in my hybrid form most, kept in that state almost entirely. Though sometimes I was sent into the arena in my fur-form or forced to receive punishment in my skin-form. In many ways I was lucky my owner didn't understand the significance of my triple tail; a small comfort.

Like the itch to fly, the itch to shift was hard to fight. Now that I had my dose of flying during our high-speed escape from Xio not two days ago, my entire being seemed consumed with the need to transform. Sune spend the majority of their lives shifting between the three forms available whenever the mood struck them. It was extremely unnatural to have been restricted as I had been for so long.

The cargo bay was dark and filled with haphazardly stacked crates and boxes. A good amount was dried food rations or so Sunder had told me but he and Tori had been working hard to catalog the other stuff in the hope that we could sell some of it or use the rest in some way. I didn't need much light to see so I made my way deeper into the bay, navigating between the mag-locked stacks to find a private place for my experiment. I didn't want anyone opening the door to see me on the off chance someone came here.

Hidden behind some of the tall stacks I briefly wondered about the wisdom of this plan before giving in to temptation. I unbuckled the leather kilt I wore and let it drop to the floor in a rush, shaking out my triple tail with some relief. I was always careful when in this form to minimize the chance that someone saw my abnormality, uncomfortable though that was.

The loincloth I wore would stay on my body when I shifted into my skin form, it was made from a stretchy flexible material. The leather skirt would fall off so I figured I'd dress again afterward when I'd managed to change my form. Optimistic, sure. A male had to be to get through these things. I couldn't let myself think about the pain to come when I tried this shift; if I did I'd surely give up.

Trying to pep myself up I had a habit of talking to myself

sometimes but it didn't matter here, in the privacy of the cargo bay. No words I spoke were going to make me feel better until I had at least tried to do this.

My ears swiveled at a small sound and for a brief moment, I worried I wasn't alone. I had good hearing and tried to locate the source of the small sound but couldn't hear a thing now. Was I so worried about being caught that I was imagining things? My guilty consciousness tricking me? Probably. There was no one here, I'd made sure to pick a moment when everyone would be in the mess hall.

I closed my eyes and focused on the familiar feeling of calling on a different form. It should be easy, I'd done these kinds of shifts dozens of times a day once upon a time. It was instinct. It was! But it wasn't right now, my body didn't want to transform when I had more than one broken and still healing bone.

The groan escaped my mouth unwanted. Pain tingled across my nerves all over my body as I fought to have my fur retreat and my body reshape. My form remained unchanged until I snapped my eyes open and looked at my unbroken arm. For a brief elated moment, I thought I had it when my face reshaped. The pain in my arm was too much, the broken arm wouldn't change shape.

In defeat I groaned, my body snapping back into my hybrid-form with a shiver. Immediately my fur stood on end, I hadn't imagined it. I wasn't alone. My eyes focused on the broken stasis pod across from me and sharpened when I saw a slight flash of movement. The glimmer of a pair of pretty blue eyes.

ABOUT THE AUTHOR

Robin O'Connor is the pen-name of an author who loves to write about strong, alien heroes and quirky heroines. She lives with her husband and son along with a couple of hundred books (hers, definitely hers) and probably just as many computer parts (her husband's). Her house therefore probably resembles something like a mad-scientist's lab on any given day.

She's always working on at least a half dozen projects at the same time but is never without time to answer questions, write up funny extras or hang out in her group online to speak with her readers.

And... please remember to leave a review, whether you liked this book or not. It helps authors to keep on writing and new readers to discover their books.

FIND HER AT:

Her website: www.robinoconnor.ink
Facebook: www.facebook.com/RobinOConnorBooks
Goodreads:
www.goodreads.com/author/show/22142455.Robin_O_Connor
Bookbub: https://www.bookbub.com/profile/robin-o-connor

ROBIN'S MAILING LIST

Want to know more about the gladiators and their future mates? Want to receive free extra bonus scenes?

Sign up for her mailing list here: robinoconnor.ink

And you'll be the first to know when her next book launches.

BOOKS BY ROBIN O'CONNOR

GLADIATORS OF THE VAGABOND SERIES

Beast Unburdened
Trickster Caught
Deviant Challenged
Feral Tamed
Healer Hunted
Stone Awakened
Doom Averted
Steel Reforged
Warrior Enchanted
Logic Broken

SERPENTS OF SERANT SERIES

The Naga Outcast's Unwanted Mate
The Naga Brute's Warrior Mate
The Naga Warlord's Virgin Mate
The Naga Maverick's Determined Mate
The Naga Scavenger's Precious Mate

STANDALONE

There's an Alien Down My Chimney
There's an Elf in My Cockpit

Printed in Great Britain
by Amazon

40526030R00138